Princesses of Palosia

Sisters torn between love and duty...

Princess Sofia and Princess Rosa have their futures mapped out for them. They've been brought up to marry well for the benefit of their country; finding a partner of their own and falling in love is not even a consideration! But when the time comes to do their royal duty, love unexpectedly finds *them*, throwing the future of their marriages—and the crown—into crisis!

Will finding true love give these princesses the courage to defy their father and fight for their own fairy-tale ending?

Find out in

Secret Royal's Napoli Reunion
by Nina Milne

Billionaire Marco doesn't even realize he's lost his heart to a princess when he falls for his long-lost love, Sofia, all over again!

And

Conveniently Engaged to a Princess
by Suzanne Merchant

The pressure is on for Rosa to marry for duty, but what happens when she unexpectedly falls in love with her convenient fiancé, Count Luca?

Both available now!

Dear Reader,

Engaged to each other from childhood, Princess Rosabella of Palosia and Conte Luca Montenale have no intention of entering into the marriage of convenience brokered by their fathers twenty years ago when they meet as adults.

Dutiful Rosa has always accepted that her future lies in marrying the man her father has chosen for her and producing a male heir, but when her half sister, Sofia, defies their father's wishes and marries for love, she changes her mind. She would rather remain single than be trapped in a loveless marriage.

Strong-willed Luca has fought against his father's obsessive control all his life, and when he discovers that he has been conveniently engaged to an unknown princess since the age of thirteen, it feels as if his dead father is manipulating him from beyond the grave. He will *never* acquiesce to this outdated agreement.

I hope you will enjoy meeting Rosa and Luca as their story unfolds on the island of Palosia, in a marble palace, magical gardens and the warm waters of the Mediterranean Sea.

Will the events of the past prevent Rosa and Luca from finding a future together?

Suzanne

CONVENIENTLY ENGAGED TO A PRINCESS

SUZANNE MERCHANT

ROMANCE

If you purchased this book without a cover you should be aware that this book is stolen property. It was reported as "unsold and destroyed" to the publisher, and neither the author nor the publisher has received any payment for this "stripped book."

Harlequin®
ROMANCE

ISBN-13: 978-1-335-47056-0

Conveniently Engaged to a Princess

Copyright © 2025 by Suzanne Merchant

Recycling programs for this product may not exist in your area.

All rights reserved. No part of this book may be used or reproduced in any manner whatsoever without written permission.

Without limiting the exclusive rights of any author, contributor or the publisher of this publication, any unauthorized use of this publication to train generative artificial intelligence (AI) technologies is expressly prohibited. Harlequin also exercises their rights under Article 4(3) of the Digital Single Market Directive 2019/790 and expressly reserves this publication from the text and data mining exception.

This is a work of fiction. Names, characters, places and incidents are either the product of the author's imagination or are used fictitiously. Any resemblance to actual persons, living or dead, businesses, companies, events or locales is entirely coincidental.

For questions and comments about the quality of this book, please contact us at CustomerService@Harlequin.com.

TM and ® are trademarks of Harlequin Enterprises ULC.

Harlequin Enterprises ULC
22 Adelaide St. West, 41st Floor
Toronto, Ontario M5H 4E3, Canada
www.Harlequin.com

HarperCollins Publishers
Macken House, 39/40 Mayor Street Upper,
Dublin 1, D01 C9W8, Ireland
www.HarperCollins.com

Printed in U.S.A.

Suzanne Merchant was born and raised in South Africa. She and her husband lived and worked in Cape Town, London, Kuwait, Baghdad, Sydney and Dubai before settling in the Sussex countryside. They enjoy visits from their three grown-up children and are kept busy attempting to wrangle two spaniels, a dachshund, a parrot and a large, unruly garden under control.

Books by Suzanne Merchant

Harlequin Romance

Their Wildest Safari Dream
Off-Limits Fling with the Billionaire
Ballerina and the Greek Billionaire
Heiress's Escape to South Africa
Cinderella's Adventure with the CEO
Best Man's Second Chance

Visit the Author Profile page at Harlequin.com.

For Jacqui
*"For there is no friend like a sister
In calm or stormy weather"*
—Christina Rossetti

Praise for Suzanne Merchant

"This is an intensely emotional and immensely satisfying read. With a few well-chosen words the author takes the reader to the heart of the African bush and into the hearts of her protagonists. I thoroughly recommend it."
—Amazon customer on *Their Wildest Safari Dream*

PROLOGUE

Luca Montenale stood still and forced down a rising tide of panic. He swiped a hand across his forehead, wiping away the sweat which stung his eyes, and turned in a slow circle. Should he go back, or should he go on? Had he last turned left, or was it right? The ancient hedges of the maze towered above him on either side, only a strip of cobalt sky visible between them. And the sun…

He squinted up at it. Heat beat down from directly overhead and that could only mean one thing: it was almost midday, the time he was supposed to present himself at his father's suite of rooms in the palace—shoes polished, hair brushed, face clean. Then they'd go to an important meeting. He hadn't been told why it was important, which was annoying, because he was thirteen and old enough to know. It was safer not to ask questions because his father was permanently in a bad mood. In fact, these days he tried not to talk to him at all.

They were going to meet the King, and he

supposed that was important enough. He'd been lectured about 'best behaviour'. As if that was necessary. He knew about good manners and holding polite conversation with adults, who were usually boring and not interested in him, even if he *was* the only son of a count whose family tree was one of the oldest, and richest, in Italy.

Not that his father had had a hand in teaching him his manners, or how to converse with kings. It was his grandparents who'd done that. But three years ago, his father had taken him away from them to live in his gloomy castle. Although he knew he was old enough not to miss them, he still did, with an ache which never went away.

He was going to be in so much trouble. If he'd been allowed to wear his jeans, instead of stupid shorts like a kid, he wouldn't have hurt his knee when he'd tripped and fallen—and that was before he'd even realised he was lost. He wished he'd never set foot in the maze, but its cool, dark shade had looked mysterious and a bit dangerous, and he'd remembered all the twists and turns he'd taken…until he hadn't.

He pulled his eyes away from the dazzling sun and raked his fingers through his hair. His father's butler, Nico—who had travelled with them from Tuscany and who had told him what clothes he had to wear—had plastered his hair to his scalp with something that smelled disgustingly of damp moss. But it had reverted to its usual thick, unruly waves, one lock flopping over his forehead. He pushed it away.

Standing in the absolute silence of a Mediterranean summer's day, he kicked at a tuft of grass and admitted to himself that he had no idea what to do.

Except the silence was not absolute. He turned his head, listening, and heard it again. Relief, quickly followed by apprehension, flooded through him. What if this was someone who'd been sent to find him? Whoever it was, they'd be angry, because he was keeping his father and, even worse, the King waiting; and angry because he was now unfit to be presented to the monarch in this dishevelled state. He pushed his hands into his pockets and told himself he didn't care.

Luca peered around the sharply trimmed edge of the hedge and huffed out a breath. This must be the middle of the maze, where water from a stone fountain trickled into a circular pond. The sound of the water had been mixed with a soft voice and now he saw to whom it belonged.

If she hadn't been the size of a four- or five-year-old girl, he'd have believed she was a fairy child—if he believed in fairies, which he didn't. She knelt on the stone bench surrounding the basin, her back to him, the grubby soles of her feet showing from beneath the skirt of the lacy white dress she wore. Her hair cascaded down her back in shimmering, fair waves and, as she leaned forward to trail her fingers across the surface of the water, she laughed.

Forgetting that he thought girls were boring, and that he was lost, Luca stepped out of the shadows into the centre of the maze.

'Who are you?' he asked.

Rosabella lifted her hand from the water and shook her fingers. Drops flew off them like a shower of sparkling diamonds and splashed into the pond. Then she turned slowly, sitting on the stone bench so that her feet dangled down but didn't reach the grass beneath them. She wriggled her toes and looked towards the voice that had asked the question.

A strange boy stood there: strange because she'd never seen him before, she thought, not strange, *peculiar*—although his clothes looked funny, and much too smart for being in the garden or playing. His white shirt had long sleeves, buttoned cuffs and a stiff collar. It looked as if it should have been tucked into his grey shorts, but one side of it hung out untidily. His socks were pulled up to his knees, one of which was grazed.

'Who are *you*? And how did you hurt your knee?'

'I asked first. And I tripped and fell.'

'Oh.'

Rosabella studied him. His hair was dark and messy, his eyes even darker, and he was tall. And he *had* asked first. She always tried to follow the rules, because that way her father wouldn't be even more angry with her than he normally was, and she also tried to be kind, because that was what her mother had taught her.

Was this boy like the one her father wished she'd been? Would she have grown tall, had hair like a raven's wing and eyes that seemed to see more than what he was looking at? Instead, she had hair which shimmered with light, like her mother's, and which seemed to annoy her father and her nurse. Everyone, really, except her half-sister, Sofia—and her eyes were plain brown.

'I'm Rosabella,' she said finally. She slipped to the ground and looked up at the boy expectantly. He looked even taller now.

'That's a pretty name. I'm Luca.'

'It means "beautiful rose", because roses are my mother's favourite flowers. Even though they have prickly stems.'

Luca took a step towards her. 'Are you prickly too?'

Rosabella giggled and shook her head. 'You're funny. People can't be prickly.'

She watched Luca glance around the space.

The high hedges of the maze enclosed it, and the only way out was the way he'd come in.

'Was it your mother you were talking to? Is she one of the gardeners?'

Rosabella shook her head again. 'She does gardening, but not today. And I wasn't talking. I was singing. To the fish.' She turned her head to look at the pond.

'The *fish*? Now *you're* funny. You can't sing to *fish*.'

Rosabella tipped up her chin. 'I can.' She turned and climbed up onto the stone bench, leaning over the water. 'I'll show you.'

Luca knelt beside her, his fingers curving around the lip of the pool, listening as Rosabella's lilting voice began to sing a song about pretty horses. Bubbles popped, and three golden fish appeared, their mouths forming round shapes on the surface of the water, almost as if they were joining in the song.

'Do they always do that, when you sing?'

He sounded astonished, and Rosa felt pleased. She nodded. 'Mmm. Sometimes the frogs sing too. But it's too hot for them now. It's midday. They're resting.'

Something she'd said made Luca jump off the bench.

'Midday! I'm going to be in such trouble.'

'Why will you be in trouble?' Anxiety clutched

at Rosabella's tummy. Trouble was something she'd been told to stay out of, and she tried her best, but sometimes it was difficult to know the difference between it and having fun.

'I'm supposed to go to a meeting, with my father, and I can't find my way out of this maze.'

The tension in Rosabella's tummy relaxed. She couldn't do anything about the time, but she could help him.

'My father also gets cross when people are late. But you aren't lost because I can show you the way.'

She reached out and took Luca's hand. 'It's easy. Come.'

CHAPTER ONE

'WHAT THE...*HELL*?'

Luca Montenale surged to his feet, sending the ornate chair crashing backwards onto the marble floor. His hands shook, making the thick, cream pages of the document he clutched between his fingers rattle.

A movement in the shadowy corridor beyond the door made him shut his mouth on a more expressive expletive. The castle staff, traumatised by the events of the past few days, had hovered around him, offering versions of what had happened and seeking reassurance, from the minute he'd stepped from the chauffeur-driven car yesterday afternoon before the ancient and massive, iron-studded front door.

He wished they'd leave him alone.

He was shocked, jet-lagged and exhausted. The trial in New York had lasted for weeks and, although he'd been sure he would win his client's case, nothing could ever be taken for granted. The verdict in their favour had been a relief, and he'd been looking forward to a quiet weekend, catching up on sleep and the newspapers, before returning to his head office in Rome.

Instead, a white-faced employee had met him at the entrance to his offices. His father, with whom he'd hardly exchanged a handful of words for over a year—and those had been angry ones—was dead. He'd taken his habitual post-lunch nap in his armchair in the drawing room and simply not woken up.

Way to go, had been Luca's first thought, hotly followed by a spike of annoyance bordering on anger. His father, the Count, the latest in a long line of custodians of this castle in Tuscany, had made his and others' lives hell for so many years, he'd hardly deserved a peaceful death.

'Sir?' The shadowy presence in the passage materialised into his father's—his *late* father's—elderly butler. He gestured towards the toppled chair. 'Is there anything…?'

Luca shook his head, as much to try to order his thoughts as to dismiss the man. 'No, thank you, Nico.' He dropped the sheaf of papers onto the desktop and waved him away.

'Very well.' Nico backed out of the door, his eyes sliding back to the chair. 'If you're sure, Count Montenale…'

Count. Luca pinched the bridge of his nose between his thumb and index finger, closing his eyes. Would he ever get used to the title? It made him feel like a different version of himself, and not one he wanted to know.

For as long as he could remember, there had been no love lost between his father and him. He might even have said for ever. His mother had died in a fall from a horse when he was two and he had no memory of her at all. It was said that his father had been furious, rather than grief-stricken. He'd forbidden her to ride the horse, but she was wilful, headstrong, and had refused to be told what she could and could not do.

'She defied me, and she paid the price,' his father had frequently said. 'I will *not* be defied.'

The iron will he'd imposed on his son when he'd summoned him back from the care of his grandparents on his tenth birthday seemed designed to crush any defiance before it started—to bend him to his will and force him into a shape closely resembling his own. Luca had fought against it with unwavering determination. He did not want to be like his father, and he had not intended to allow him to dictate how he lived his life. It seemed unjust that a man could determine how his son lived just because generations of sons before him had followed the same path.

His grandparents had been kind, fair and loving, always trying to help others. He wanted to be like *them*.

As soon as he'd been old enough, he'd broken

away. Able to use the fortune his mother had bequeathed him, which his father could not touch, he'd gained the qualifications he wanted and climbed to the top of the legal profession with astonishing speed. He defended the defenceless when he could, and stood up for the rights of men and women whose voices would not otherwise be heard.

His father had never forgiven him for leaving the family estate. He'd accused him of abandoning his family, bringing shame on the ancient name of Montenale, and had hinted at retribution.

Luca rubbed his eyes and looked up at the massive portrait that dominated the room. His father returned his stare. The artist had captured his likeness admirably: the silver mane of hair swept back from the broad forehead; the frown between the heavy brows; the imperious nose and the mouth set in a straight, fierce line. But the eyes were the most compelling element of the picture. Deep and dark, they glared at Luca, and the expression they held seemed to be one of thinly-veiled triumph.

It took an effort of will, but he dragged his gaze away from those eyes and back to the document he'd dropped. He might have broken free of his father's control in life, but there on the burgundy leather top, signed and stamped with the thick, wax seal of the Montenale dynasty, lay the evidence that his control reached to trap him from beyond the grave.

Luca heaved the chair from the floor and sat

down at the desk again. He gathered up the pages, which he'd found filed away with his father's papers, and ran his practised eye over them, even though he'd known what he'd find from the instant he'd read the first paragraph.

Twenty years ago, when Luca had been thirteen, his father had signed a contract promising him in marriage to Princess Rosabella of Palosia on the occasion of her twenty-fifth birthday. Scanning the print, which wavered and swam in his shocked vision, he calculated that date to be in three months' time.

He shoved the papers away and flung himself back in the chair, massaging the back of his neck where the rigid muscles felt as hard as iron. The whole idea was so preposterous as to be laughable, except that he knew it was deadly serious. This was a legal document, and it would take delicate negotiations to extricate himself from its grip.

He would never agree to a marriage of convenience. Such a thing went against the moral convictions on which he'd founded his career: freedom of choice, the importance of being heard and the defence of the persecuted. Neither he nor his proposed bride had been given a choice in this matter, or the opportunity to voice their opinions on it. To agree to it would undermine him professionally. He'd be regarded as a hypocrite and his career would be compromised.

Was this the threat his father had hinted at during their furious arguments? At least, Luca thought grimly, his sudden death had robbed him of the opportunity to gloat at his son.

The clearest memory Luca had of his visit to the kingdom of Palosia was of meeting the little daughter of one of the gardeners. She'd led him, unerringly, out of the maze when he was lost. He'd been reprimanded by Nico for being late, had his shoes cleaned, his painful knee scrubbed and been told to brush his hair, before being handed over to his angry father and ushered into the austere presence of King Fiero.

Later that day they'd returned to Tuscany. His father had seemed to be in a rare good mood on the flight and had ordered champagne. Now Luca knew why.

He flipped open his laptop and emailed his PA in Rome, asking her to investigate flights to Palosia, before composing a letter to King Fiero, requesting a meeting. He could have undertaken this awkward task by email, but good manners dictated that he should do the King the courtesy of meeting him face to face. The visit shouldn't take more than a few hours and he would only need to meet the King. It was simply a matter of unravelling a business deal, and there was no reason at all why he should meet the princess.

CHAPTER TWO

Princess Rosabella checked her watch. There was enough time to plant out the three remaining lavender plants into the herb garden. She firmed the rich, dark earth around them and then rose to her feet, bending to brush dust from her skirt. She stretched, easing muscles which were stiff after spending the morning bent over the flowerbeds.

The gardens surrounding the gleaming white palace on the hill fell away in ordered terraces. Flowers bloomed in a riot of colour, roses scrambling over pergolas and archways. The hedges of the maze—one of the original features of the gardens which had survived centuries of neglect—formed a dark-green block of linear orderliness amongst the vibrant exuberance of summer.

Lifting her eyes, Rosa could see the jumble of pastel-coloured houses of the nearest village clustered in the valley, while above them rose forest-clad mountains, their peaks shimmering in the heat. A sliver of sparkling sea glinted in the distance.

The sultry stillness was broken only by the sound of trickling water from one of the many fountains and rills that dotted the gardens, and the harsh call of a bird of prey, just visible, riding the thermals high above her.

Later, when the afternoon had cooled, she'd return to water the plants. She'd need the solace of the garden then. Before that could happen, she'd have to endure what was sure to be a massively awkward lunch meeting with her parents and the man they thought was going to take her off their hands, be her husband and provide a male heir to the kingdom.

She'd dreaded this day ever since her father, the King, had told her that her husband-to-be was coming to meet her and, subject to the paperwork being put in order, there was no reason why their wedding shouldn't take place as soon as she turned twenty-five in September.

'But we've only just had Sofia's wedding,' she'd argued, and then wished she'd said nothing. The subject of her half-sister's marriage was guaranteed to anger her father. She'd shunned the men he'd chosen for her and instead had married for love. The King had grudgingly agreed to allow the wedding to take place on Palosia; and, even though it was not a Palosian tradition,

Sofia had insisted on having Rosabella by her side as her bridesmaid.

Rosabella knew that the brave face the King had put on events had been a perilously fragile mask. He regarded Sofia's defiance of his wishes as a loss of face on his part, but she was loved by the people, and he'd feared a backlash of negative public opinion if he denied her the wedding on Palosia she so badly wanted.

Rosabella had hoped to gain more time, because the longer her marriage was delayed, the greater the chance that something might happen to prevent it. And then she wouldn't have to tell her father that like Sofia, she refused to enter into a marriage of convenience. The idea of confronting him with this bombshell terrified her. She needed more time to gather her courage to do it.

'You, Rosabella,' he'd replied, disdain colouring every syllable, 'Are my *second* daughter, of my *second* wife. It's not as though you can expect this marriage to be a celebration. It's a legal contract between two people.' His hand had swept downwards in a dismissive gesture. 'Nothing more.'

Rosabella understood only too well what this marriage would be. And, if she hadn't, his use of the word *second* would have told her all she needed to know. Second-best was all she'd ever amount to. Her father had made sure she'd always known that she held no power and could not expect any man to want her for herself. Born a girl, she was of no use to him whatsoever until she produced a son. By ancient law, women could not rule the country, but they could produce a male heir.

She should consider herself fortunate that he'd been able to broker any marriage for her at all. A rich Italian count, the inhabitant of one of the most beautiful castles in Tuscany surrounded by ancient and productive vineyards, had wanted more than he already had. The allure of connecting his family to the royal line of Palosia had been too much for him to resist, and he'd promised his son as her husband long before her father had ingrained in her the knowledge that she completely lacked beauty or grace.

It would be an important alliance, her father had said. Rosabella knew that what he hadn't said was much more pertinent. Once married to the so-far nameless and faceless son of the Count, she would be taken away from the only life she'd ever known. Her mother, despised by the King for not producing a son, would be left without the protection which until now Rosabella had provided.

Rosabella flicked her long braid over her shoulder and tugged her straw hat low over her eyes. While her mother had always encouraged her to spend time in the garden, learning about the wonders of the natural world and benefiting from the effects of fresh air and sunshine, she'd been a stickler for making sure her fair skin was protected.

She glanced down at her hands and frowned at her nails, which were ringed with dried earth. Sighing, she dropped her garden trowel and fork into her basket and turned towards the Queen's private quarters. She could already imagine the exclamation of horror that she knew her mother's lady in waiting, Luisa, would utter when she saw her. It was going to take every minute of the hour she had left to make herself look presentable for her future husband. Except, he wasn't her future husband, because she was going to refuse to marry him, or anyone else of her father's choosing.

From the age of four, Rosabella had been told by her father that she would marry the man he'd chosen for her and be grateful for it. She was too chubby, he'd said, when anyone praised her round, rosy cheeks. Too tall, he'd spat, when she'd reached a height from which she could look him straight in the eye. Too thin, he'd sneered, when the hand-me-down dresses from her half-sister had had to be adjusted to fit her. And she was too fair—just like her mother, he'd added.

What red-blooded man would want a fair, slip

of a girl who looked as if she might break if touched? No-one, that was certain. He knew, because he'd learned that lesson from marrying her mother.

All these faults would have been regarded as assets if she'd been the boy her father had so badly needed. As a child, she'd tried her best to please him, desperate to make up for not being what he'd wanted her to be. If she rode her pony fearlessly, dived from a high rock into the sea or hit a tennis ball with all her might, surely he'd notice, pay her attention or perhaps even praise her?

But he'd simply snapped at her to try to be ladylike, because he didn't know what he'd do with her if the marriage he'd arranged fell through. There was no chance at all of finding anyone else who would be willing to take her for his wife.

She'd understood from an early age that she had to do as he wished even though her parents' marriage was a disastrous example. Her father lived in a perpetual state of simmering anger, and her mother had retreated to her quarters years ago and took hardly any part in the life of the palace. Her failure to produce a son and heir had come to define her, and her relationship with the King, and she'd poured her energies into restoring the neglected palace gardens and setting up charities to promote education for women and children.

Rosa accepted that her marriage of convenience could only ever be loveless. After all, if her own father could not bring himself to love her, what hope was there that a perfect stranger might feel differently? Absolutely none. Although her mother cared for her, and told her she was beautiful, it was her father's admiration, attention and *love* which she'd craved so fiercely. When she married the son of the Italian count, would her father finally be pleased with her? *Only if you produce a son*, a voice whispered in her head. And, even then, it would not be his daughter he'd be pleased with, but his grandson.

Everything had changed for Rosabella when her beloved half-sister had rebelled. She'd refused to marry the man of their father's choice and had run away, to find her mother who'd abandoned her as a baby and been banished by the King. And then she'd married the man she loved. *Truly loved.*

Rosabella shivered, despite the heat that bounced off the cobblestones between the beds of herbs. The joy and emotion that radiated from her sister and her new husband seemed magical. This was how two people marrying each other should look, she realised. They had eyes only for each other. The glances they shared, the gentle touch of his hand on her arm and the sense that they might set each other alight with the warmth of their feelings had showed Rosa a whole world which she hadn't dreamed existed. In the depths of her soul she knew that no man would ever—*could* ever—love her like that and she'd made up her mind, then and there, that she would never marry.

The reality of a loveless, convenient match suddenly felt abhorrent. She'd glimpsed the love between Sofia and Marco and she would never settle for anything less. She'd rather continue to work in the garden and protect her mother from her father's wrath than do a strange man's bidding in a foreign castle, away from everything she knew and loved.

How she would ever find the courage to tell her father of her decision was something she hadn't been able to think about, but now, with her potential husband here, the problem had become urgent.

The King had ruled her life, and that of her half-sister, with an iron rod. Never once had she defied his will. The idea made her stomach churn with anxiety. She was terrified of his anger, which she knew would be incandescent. What if he banished her, as he'd done to Sofia and her mother? What if he prevented her from ever seeing her own mother again? Apprehension crawled over her skin. Somewhere she was going to have to find the strength to face up to him and tell him she was ruining his plans.

Sofia had found that courage, strengthened by love. Unlovable as Rosa was, would she be able to emulate her?

Precious minutes slipped away while she stood, staring at the view, lost in fearful thought. Being late for an appointment with King Fiero was unthinkable. Rosabella picked up her basket of tools and broke into an unladylike run, plunging through the arch into the dim shadow of the courtyard.

Luca did not see what hit him. The bright sunlight striking the white marble paving was dazzling, even though he wore sunglasses. He'd decided to take a stroll through the palace gardens before lunch. He remembered the maze and smiled to himself, deciding to avoid it. The little girl who'd helped him escape all those years ago would be grown up now, as he was, and no longer singing to the fish.

The impact almost knocked the breath from his lungs. There was a crash that sounded like metal objects hitting the marble slabs, and a cry. Acting purely on impulse, Luca's hands clamped around a pair of slender arms. The owner of them swayed and he tightened his hold.

'Hey,' he said, 'Are you alright?' He risked

releasing one of the arms then raised a hand to remove his shades and slip them into a trouser pocket. Hands pushed firmly against his chest, and he looked down.

'Yes, thank you, I'm alright.' The voice was breathy and definitely feminine and he could feel the rapid rise and fall of her chest against his shirt. 'I'm late. If you'll excuse me…'

'Of course.' Luca dropped his hands and stepped back, putting a little distance between them, but registering how pleasant her nearness had felt for those few seconds and how delicious she smelled—of lavender and warm sunshine.

The woman swiped a forearm across her forehead, leaving a streak of dirt. She glanced around, then crouched, gathering up her trowel and fork and reaching for the straw hat that had bounced off her head.

'Allow me.' Luca quickly bent to help her. Her fair hair fell in a thick braid over her shoulder, and in the vee at the neck of her linen smock he caught a glimpse of smooth skin. As they stood, she raised her eyes to meet his.

He felt as if he'd been hit again, in the stomach this time. He narrowed his gaze and studied her face. What were the chances? He did a quick mental calculation. She looked about the right age. Her long fair hair was tamed in a braid, but her eyes... He was sure they were the same wide-spaced, soft brown eyes he remembered.

So she'd grown up to be a gardener. He supposed her mother had retired by now and she'd taken over her duties. He shook his head slightly, not quite believing the coincidence of meeting her again so many years later.

'Thank you.' She was turning away but something made him want to keep her there for another minute.

'You're...you're still here.'

She turned back and a puzzled expression clouded her eyes—those brown eyes.

'What do you mean? Do I know you?'

'Yes. That is, I *think* we met a long time ago.'

A frown creased the skin between her brows. 'I... I'm sorry. I don't remember you.'

Luca pulled a hand across the back of his neck and shook his head. 'No, you probably don't. You were just a little girl, but you led me out of the maze when I was lost.'

She nibbled her bottom lip, her eyes on his face. 'Oh. Perhaps I do remember something about that. It *was* a long time ago. You said you were...*in trouble*?'

'Twenty years,' he said decisively. 'It was twenty years ago. You're...your name is...' He searched his memory. 'Something to do with roses?'

Her face cleared and she smiled slightly, the

faint indentation of a dimple showing in her left cheek.

'Yes, it is. But, if you'll excuse me, I'm already late.' She held her basket in one hand and the brim of her battered straw hat in the other. 'I'm sorry I crashed into you.' She stepped backwards, away from him. 'Thank you for helping me.'

'You sang to the fish,' he said. 'It was a song about pretty horses.' The memory surprised him, surfacing from nowhere.

A smile lit her face, the dimple deepening. 'Yes,' she said. 'It probably was.'

With that, she walked quickly away. She placed the basket on a stone bench, tugged open a pair of French windows and disappeared.

Luca watched until she'd vanished into the dark interior of the palace, the door clicking shut behind her. After a moment he pulled out his sunglasses again and walked through the archway into the garden.

The hazy memories of his previous visit to Palosia suddenly shifted into sharper focus.

Rosabella turned and backed away from the French windows until she was sure she couldn't be seen from the courtyard—or, to be specific, seen by the tall, dark-haired stranger who stood there and appeared to be watching her.

She wondered who he could be, and she puzzled over the fact that he'd remembered her after their chance meeting...had he said *twenty* years ago? Perhaps being lost in the maze had frightened him as a boy and the incident was burned into his memory. Maybe he'd been visiting the King with his father and had now become an envoy in his own right, here to discuss some political matter.

She had no idea about affairs of state. Whenever she'd showed an interest in anything to do with the governing of Palosia, the opinions of the people or the preservation of the precious, unique natural habitats of the island, she'd been slapped down and reminded to confine herself to matters befitting a girl.

If her father needed proof that she was unladylike and lacking even the smallest amount of decorum, she'd just provided it. Not to run, when she should walk, was one of the first points of etiquette she'd ever been taught. Crashing into a visitor with enough force to almost knock him off his feet and the air from her own lungs must rank amongst the most cardinal of sins. Luckily, he'd kept her upright. Falling in a heap at his feet would have been even more undignified and embarrassing. She rubbed at her upper arms where the warmth of his hands lingered and wondered why, in the moments when she'd been pressed against him, she'd felt somehow protected and safe. It wasn't a familiar feeling.

As she watched, he pulled his shades from a pocket and put them on, then disappeared through the archway.

Rosabella heel-toed her dusty rope-soled espadrilles from her feet and wriggled her toes. The quick tap of footsteps approached along the passage.

'Princess Rosabella? I've been searching for you. Wherever have you been? The time...'

Rosabella turned, ready to face the worst. 'I was in the garden, Luisa. I needed to...'

'Oh!' Luisa stopped, dismay spreading across her habitually impassive, unshockable features. 'Well, I shouldn't have expected anything different, I suppose, but just this once I thought...' Her tone was resigned. 'Never mind now; come along, we don't have much time.'

She glanced at the tall grandfather clock that ticked steadily in an alcove, eating up the seconds. 'We'll just have to make the best of it.' She shook her head, and Rosabella felt a needling of guilt. Her dirty fingernails and messy hair that resisted being tamed wouldn't make things easy for Luisa.

'You mean the best of *me*. I'm sorry, Luisa. I thought I had enough time, but...'

Luisa pursed her lips. 'I've known you all your

life, Rosabella. When have you ever had enough time to do everything you wanted to do in the garden, especially when there was something else waiting which you *didn't* want to do?'

Rosabella pushed her hands into the pockets of her skirt, hoping Luisa hadn't seen her nails, and studied her grimy bare feet. 'What do you mean?' Was she *that* transparent? She'd tried hard to hide her feelings about the impending ordeal.

'I mean this meeting with your parents. I know you've been dreading it.'

Rosabella nodded. 'Yes, you're right, I *have* been dreading it. But, now that it's here, or rather *he* is here, I *do* want to do this. I want to get it out of the way as quickly as possible.'

CHAPTER THREE

Luca followed the stiff-backed courtier from the magnificent suite of rooms he'd been given in what he presumed to be the guest wing of the palace. Deep carpets muffled their footsteps until they emerged into a soaring atrium with marble-clad walls and tiled floors decorated with jewel-coloured mosaics. They crossed the space beneath a crystal chandelier and entered an antechamber of even greater opulence. Rich rugs cushioned the floor and light reflected from a dozen gilded surfaces.

The man ahead of him bowed. 'His Majesty, King Fiero of Palosia,' he announced. 'Sir, I present the Conte Luca Montenale.' He stepped back smartly.

The King, who stood beside a wide, ornately carved desk, extended his right hand.

'Welcome.' He inclined his head and it seemed to be with an afterthought that he turned slightly and indicated the presence of a pale, anxious-looking woman who hovered near the windows, as if uncertain of her place. 'Her Majesty, Queen Chiara,' he said.

Luca bowed over the King's hand, and then towards the Queen. 'An honour,' he murmured, hiding his surprise at her presence at this meeting. Perhaps she would withdraw after this initial introduction. Moreover, the King seemed far from pleased to see him. Deep lines furrowed his forehead, and his lips were pressed together in an angry, straight line.

Had he somehow discovered that Luca was here to cancel the marriage of convenience, rather than to act on it? That was impossible. Luca had told nobody the reason for his visit to this island state, or even of the existence of the marriage contract. Had he displeased him in some other way? Perhaps his late father...

Suddenly, Luca wished he'd taken a little time to consider his actions rather than rushing in uncharacteristic haste to a meeting with this formidable man. But he'd been so shocked to discover what his father had done, and so keen to disentangle himself from its implications, that he'd wanted to resolve the issue and free himself without delay.

But King Fiero's daughter would soon be twenty-five and he would be ready to put plans in place for their marriage. He would have been anticipating this moment for the past twenty years.

He was going to be furious, disappointed and, quite possibly, feel humiliated. And his daughter, the princess, would have been anticipating this day almost all her life.

Zipped into a compartment of his luggage was the original contract, and now he wished he'd studied it in greater detail, as he realised he didn't even know her name. For a man like him, reading and understanding the detail of every case or transaction was of paramount importance. This was an embarrassing omission, and he felt ashamed. He'd never believed in making excuses for sloppy behaviour. He could only think that the shock of his father's death, coupled with the discovery that he was promised in marriage to an unknown foreign princess, had affected his usually razor-sharp and incisive mind and prompted him to act in such an out-of-character, impulsive fashion.

King Fiero's eyes remained fixed on his face. 'My condolences on the death of your father.'

'Thank you.' Luca nodded.

'My daughter is late,' the King rasped. 'I apologise. I'll…'

'Your *daughter*?' Luca sucked in a breath. He hadn't expected the King's daughter—Luca's supposed future *wife*—or the Queen to be present at this meeting. Once again, he berated himself for not having been more measured in his approach; for not having made clear that he'd only expected to meet the King on this brief visit, to pave the way towards cancelling the agreement his father had made on his behalf.

Presenting facts had never been a problem for him, but this was different. His decision would impact on the lives of the King, Queen and their daughter in a negative way. It was never going to be easy, but conducting the discussion in the presence of the Queen and the princess would make it much more difficult.

'Yes, my daughter, whom you are going to marry.'

Luca imagined that the girl's options were limited, if her father had been determined to settle her future from such an early age. He felt a twinge of guilt at what he was about to do. The princess's dreams of marriage would lie in ruins when he walked away from this meeting. His guilt was followed by a surge of anger towards his father, who had brought about this whole, disastrous situation. Nevertheless, he would not allow sentiment to cloud his judgement or alter his decision.

Luca heard the click and swish of a door opening. The King turned and the Queen's gaze, which had been fixed on a spot on the floor, moved towards the sound.

He turned his head.

A young woman sank into a low curtsey before the King, her head bowed.

'You're late,' snapped the monarch.

'Your Majesty, I apologise...'

'Get up.'

There was a soft whisper of silk as the fine, pale green fabric of her dress settled about her hips. It fell from a fitted bodice into gentle folds, to just above her ankles. A conservative, high neckline, and sleeves that reached her wrists, only served to direct his attention to the soft curves that were tantalisingly visible beneath the fabric—curves which he could, all too easily, imagine pressed against his own hard, honed body.

Your Majesty? Was this woman seriously expected to address her father with such stiff formality? And the King's tone had been harsh to the point of displaying blatant dislike.

Another wave of guilt assailed him. Perhaps he, as her promised husband, was her only hope of escaping what appeared to be a tyrannical father.

Her slender neck was bent, her eyes downcast. Thick, fair hair formed a glossy, complicated knot dotted with seed-pearl clips in the nape of her neck. Larger pearls gleamed in her earlobes. She appeared to be composed, but the way her long fingers plucked at her skirt hinted at anxiety.

'Up,' repeated the King.

The movement as she stood was smooth and practised. She clasped her hands together in front of her and raised her head.

For the second time in two hours, Luca felt as if the air had been punched from his lungs. He tried to breathe in, but his shirt and suit jacket suddenly felt tight and restrictive. He wished he could loosen his tie. What had happened to the oxygen in the vast room? Could he request that a window be opened? His head spun, his brain trying to find a logical explanation for this feeling of confusion but coming up with nothing.

Because the brown eyes fringed with long lashes that had lifted to his face and then dropped again were unmistakeably those of the little girl who'd sung a song to the fish about pretty horses... and of the grown-up gardener who had crashed into him earlier in the day, sending her tools and hat flying.

No wonder he could imagine the soft contours of her body pressed against his own. Less than two hours ago, that was exactly where they'd been. Their body-to-body contact might only have lasted a few seconds, but the pleasure of it had been imprinted firmly on his memory.

The King's voice sounded distant, and Luca fought to engage his brain to make sense of his words.

'My daughter, Princess Rosabella…'

Rosabella. He remembered her name now. *It's because they're my mother's favourite flowers.*

Finally, he found his voice, but the only words his brain could come up with were far from the courteous, formal ones that would have been expected.

'It's you,' he said.

If her father expected her to curtsey to this man, he was going to be disappointed in her yet again. Rosabella engaged all the strength of her core muscles to stop herself from swaying on her feet. Silently, she gave thanks for the fact that she'd won the argument over her shoes. Luisa had favoured cream courts with a heel—high enough to lend some sophistication to her outfit—but Rosabella had insisted on wearing the pale-gold ballet flats. They were comfortable and safe, and today she needed comfort and safety as she never had before.

She'd had many years to imagine what her intended husband might be like. When she'd asked her father if she might see a photograph of him, he'd brushed her request aside with an irritated flick of his hand.

At first, when she'd been much younger, she'd thought he might be a dashing prince, or a knight, who would ride a white horse, sweep her off her feet and carry her away on his galloping steed, like in one of the stories she'd loved to read.

But as she'd grown up and reality had taken hold, she'd imagined he must be small and weak—a man who bent to his father's will, as she did, never permitted to express an opinion or follow his own path. Surely only such a man would have agreed to marry her when she had nothing to offer beyond her royal lineage?

Never had her imagination been so far off the mark. She kept her eyes downcast and gripped a fistful of the silk of her dress in each hand.

How could this man be her intended husband? There must be some mistake. This was the man she'd collided with not two hours ago, who'd held her arms and stopped her from falling, and against whose hard, broad body she'd been pinned for a few brief, confusing seconds.

She wanted to release her grip on her dress and feel the place on her upper arms where his strong hands had supported her, but she was frozen with shock.

Could it be true that they had met twenty years ago when he'd been lost in the maze? It must be, or how else would he know that she'd sung her favourite lullaby to the fish?

The silence in the room seemed to stretch and shrink around her, becoming more brittle by the second, and she knew her father would expect her to do something to break it...but what?

She'd wanted to get this meeting over with. She'd made her decision to refuse to go ahead with the marriage, and she'd needed to tell her father while she was being propelled forwards on a wave of resolve. But in that brief instant, when her eyes had met the dark ones of the man in front of her, her determination had shaken and shattered around her.

This was not a man marrying her because his father had decided on it, or because he had no other choice. His broad-shouldered stance, confident demeanour and direct, take-no-prisoners stare would have given him the pick of hundreds of eligible, beautiful women, and the choice would be his alone. Neither his father, nor anyone else, would influence him. If he chose her, it would be a true marriage of convenience, solely on his terms. She had nothing to give him but her name. If he married her, it would be because it suited him. There could be no other explanation.

These thoughts tumbled through Rosabella's head as she stared at the floor, her heart thundering in her chest and her blood pounding in her ears.

It's you, he'd said. Had that been disappointment? Surprise? *Disbelief?* Or all three?

'*Rosabella!*' The King's voice cracked across

the silence, harsh with displeasure. 'Where are your manners?'

Her head snapped up. 'I... I'm...'

'This is Count Luca Montenale. Please greet him appropriately.' She saw her father turn towards the Count, his slight shrug seeming to say, *I've done my best. It's over to you.*

Rosabella forced herself to take a deep, necessary breath. Consciously she relaxed her tense fingers and smoothed the crumpled fabric of her dress. She straightened her spine, raised her chin and dared to seek out those dark eyes again.

There was no disappointment in their depths. There was surprise, certainly, and a trace of disbelief. But what else she found—which astonished her—was his look of interest, as if he wanted to know how the little, bare-footed girl in the maze and the grown-up woman who looked like a gardener could possibly be the princess, his future wife.

'What do you mean, "it's you"?' barked the King. 'Have you met before? How? When...?'

One corner of the Count's mouth kicked up; had she imagined it or had that slight movement of his head been a deliberate shake of denial?

We'll keep it between ourselves.

She understood his meaning as clearly as if he'd spoken the words out loud. As if he knew exactly how her father would react to being told he'd found her, bare-footed, singing to the fish; and that she'd cannoned into him while running in an unladylike manner, late for this meeting.

He reached out and lifted her hand, bowing low over it so that his dark head hid from the King's view the fact that he brushed the pad of his thumb in a feather-light touch across her knuckles.

She might have found the gesture forward or presumptuous, but instead his touch filled her with reassurance, as if to say she could feel safe with him and he understood some of the turmoil of her thoughts.

He held her hand for mere seconds, then straightened up and let it go. Glancing towards the King, he moved to her side and offered her his arm, instead.

'Forgive me, Your majesty,' he said, his voice smooth. 'I simply meant I've waited a long time to meet your daughter. Come, Your Highness.' He inclined his head towards the doors that stood open at the far end of the room, beyond which lay the terrace and the view down the tree-lined walk towards the fountains. 'Perhaps you and I need to take time to get to know each other a little.'

Rosabella looked at her father to see how he had reacted to the Count's suggestion. Would he feel sidelined and therefore furious? He probably wanted this marriage to go ahead badly enough not to display any anger towards her future husband. He'd reserve that for later, when she'd disappoint him yet again by failing to produce a son, just as her mother had.

A movement made her look towards the windows, and for the first time she became aware of her mother's presence. She'd taken a step forward and raised a hand, as if about to say something. But her hand fluttered down to her side again and she dipped her head, avoiding Rosabella's eyes.

For as long as she could remember, Rosabella's mother had warned her against believing any man who made promises of everlasting love and happiness. She'd said she knew, from her own bitter experience, that such promises would always either be conditional or simply untrue. If Rosabella doubted her advice, all she needed to do was reflect on how her father, the King, treated her. Her earliest memories were coloured by his words of disdain and disapproval. In withholding the fatherly love she'd craved, he'd convinced her that she was unworthy of any love at all.

The Queen's ancient, noble family had fallen on hard times when she'd been a girl and her father had seen a way back to fortune through marrying his daughter into the royal family of Palosia. The King, furious at the betrayal of his first wife, had divorced her and married Chiara with almost unseemly haste. He'd promised to adore her for ever and had showered her with luxurious gifts. Chiara's upbringing had been sheltered and she had been raised to be a dutiful daughter and wife. She'd had no reason to doubt the promises made to her.

But the King's adoration had been conditional on Chiara producing a son to inherit the throne. The birth of Rosabella had been traumatic, almost costing the Queen her life and robbing her of the ability to have more children.

Thwarted again in his plan to produce an heir, the King had quickly turned away from his wife and disappointing baby daughter, moving them to an isolated wing of the palace and made sure their paths crossed as infrequently as possible.

The Queen had raised Rosabella to be meek and obedient, but she had not tried to shield her from her own disillusionment with the idea of love and the institution of marriage. She'd explained that the King regarded Rosabella as nothing more than a useful commodity, a bargaining tool that he had used in arranging a marriage of convenience for her. She would have to go through with the marriage, but she must enter into it with no expectation of love.

This tall man who now stood beside her, with the broad shoulders, solid, sheltering chest, the deep, dark eyes which seemed to look into her soul and read her emotions and the firm yet sensuous mouth which had hinted at a smile, was the last person on earth whom she could, or should, trust. He might try to convince her that she was safe with him but believing him would lead her straight into a position of weakness and disappointment.

His agenda was obvious: he wanted to separate her from the presence of her parents so that he could ply her with empty promises of devotion and duty. She sent a swift glance of gratitude towards her mother, even though her eyes remained downcast. The Count's gallantry had made her drop her guard for a few dangerous moments, but the memories of her mother's warnings had brought her to her senses.

He didn't want to get to know her at all. Why would he? Legally, she was his already. There was just the wedding itself which had to happen before he could take her away to his castle in Tuscany. Once there, he would hope she would quickly produce a son, which would mean he'd be free to carry on with the life of his choice, leaving her isolated, just as her mother had been.

If she refused to marry the Count, what could her father do? He would be furious, but she was prepared for that. He could send her away. That idea made her tummy drop and her heart race with fear, especially if it meant she could no longer see her mother, but she would have to find the courage to face it.

He could make her life hard and unhappy, but entering into a loveless marriage, far from everything she held dear, would be worse. Her parents' own marriage was the perfect example.

The one thing he could not do was force her to say, 'I do'. That knowledge was the most powerful weapon she possessed.

So instead of taking the Count's proffered arm, Rosabella folded her hands together in front of her. She lifted her chin a fraction and took a step away from him.

'No,' she said, audibly this time. 'I don't think we do.'

CHAPTER FOUR

Luca kept his expression impassive. He inclined his head.

'As you wish.'

When their eyes had met, he'd seen her surprise and confusion, but he thought he'd also seen something like...*hope*? Was that because she believed he would rescue her from what seemed to be a toxic atmosphere in this palace? It might be sumptuous and beautiful, set like a glittering jewel in the lush landscape of Palosia, but the reality of it was cold and forbidding, lacking in any feeling of welcoming warmth or friendliness. Life within its boundaries, in spite of all the comforts and the vibrant gardens, might feel like a prison.

Whatever he'd seen was quickly obscured, like a camera shutter dropping down over her eyes or an inner light being extinguished. She'd stiffened as he'd moved beside her, as if she found the idea of his touch frightening or distasteful.

He remembered how she'd crashed into him

earlier, and the firm, almost desperate way she'd thrust herself away from him. As he'd walked along the garden paths afterwards, between the flowerbeds alive with the sound of bees, beneath the trees where birds sang, his thoughts had been on her, rather than on his surroundings. He'd puzzled over her reaction. Had she been embarrassed that she, a palace gardener, had collided with a stranger and possible guest of the King?

Now that he knew who she was, he was more intrigued than ever. What had happened to the beguiling and enchanting girl who'd taken his hand so readily in the maze, to make her shrink from the touch of a man—even just a touch that had been accidental and stopped her from falling onto the paved courtyard?

Luca had never been short of female attention, or lacked the company of a beautiful woman when he'd needed one on his arm. But his career had taken precedence over any desire for a lasting commitment. Having broken the ties with his father, he'd had to prove that he'd done the right thing. He'd been disillusioned by many of the women he'd met. Their interest in him seemed driven by what he was worth and what he would one day inherit, rather than in what drove him to do what he did, and his commitment to defending the disenfranchised.

Bitterly, he reflected on the fact that the only

interest his father had shown in him over the past ten years had been to enquire occasionally whether or not he was in any sort of relationship. What would have happened if the answer had been yes? How would his father have informed him that he was not free to marry a woman of his choice because he'd been unknowingly engaged to a princess since the age of thirteen?

He should be glad that the Princess Rosabella had given him the cold shoulder, he thought wryly. If she was indifferent to his attentions, it would make the task of telling the King he could never marry her that much easier.

But something didn't feel right. He watched her as she exchanged a murmured word with her mother. Her spine was ramrod-straight, her head held high. The hem of her silk dress swung, brushing against her legs—legs that looked as stiff as poles.

Her body language spoke of conflict and anxiety rather than of any pleasure or excitement. He thought of the wide smile she'd given him when he'd reminded her about singing to the fish, and how she'd swung away, carrying her basket and hat.

If he hadn't seen that version of her, he wouldn't have believed it existed. It was as if, in scrubbing away the dirt of the garden, putting on her silk dress and taming her hair into a regal style scattered with pearls she'd dressed herself in a layer of protective armour which held her in its stiff, formal shape.

And protected her from her father. Or from her prospective husband. An irrational desire to discover the secrets behind the impassive mask of her face took him by surprise.

He'd planned to spend no more than one night on the island, extricating himself from the net in which his father had seen fit to entangle him. But the flash of unguarded emotion in Rosabella's eyes when she'd recognised him told him that something much more complex and intriguing lay beneath the face she was willing to show him, now that she knew who he was.

She'd shut it down quickly, but not quickly enough. He'd built his professional reputation on his ability to read people. The merest flicker of an expression glimpsed across a crowded court room could give him the lead he needed to probe a defendant's story, getting them to unwittingly reveal something vital in a case.

He pushed his hands into his pockets and lifted a shoulder, casting a deliberately rueful glance towards the King. *Just give her time*, his look implied. His fingers flexed. The sudden image he had of removing those pearls and feeling her silky hair between his fingers surprised and irritated him. This was no time for the inconvenient, unexpected desire that tightened his muscles and pushed up his heart rate. He was here to escape from the deal in which his father had tied him up—*damn him and his obsessive need for control*—not to entertain thoughts of seduction.

If Rosabella didn't want his attention, he would never force it on her—or any woman, for that matter. But he felt a connection to her which he could not explain and he wanted to explore it.

The King frowned and shot an angry glance at his daughter's back. A flick of his hand acknowledged the uniformed man who stood at the door.

'Your Majesties, Your Highness, my Lord— lunch is served.'

For Rosabella, the formal lunch couldn't end quickly enough.

She'd expected to be seated next to the Count. Instead, they were placed opposite one another, meaning there was no escaping the gaze of those dark eyes, which she suspected saw far too much.

She pushed food around her plate, every mouthful she attempted tasting like sawdust, needing a gulp of wine to wash it down.

'What's the matter with you?' hissed the King, while Luca's attention was taken up with trying to engage the Queen in conversation. 'Eat.'

Rosabella turned sharply towards him, angry at his words and tone, but knowing she could never let it show. 'I'm not a child, sir. And I'm not hungry.'

'You're behaving like a spoilt teenager. I don't care if you're hungry or not.'

'Your Highness.' The deep, authoritative voice made Rosabella turn her attention back to the Count. 'Allow me to speak for the Princess Rosabella. This occasion is an unusual one, for both of us. It's not surprising if she's lost her appetite.'

Secretly grateful for his intervention, Rosabella watched as his strong fingers closed around the delicate stem of his wine glass. He raised it and took a mouthful. Why did she find it impossible to drag her eyes away from the smooth skin of his throat as he swallowed? How could such a simple, ordinary action feel...sensuous?

He replaced the glass on the table, and she realised he'd been watching her from beneath his lowered lids. Now he raised them and she felt the full force of his gaze. She tried to pull her eyes away, but he'd captured them in his, trapping her. Her cheeks heated and she knew her discomfort would be clearly displayed in the flush she could feel seeping across her pale skin.

The impossible idea that she should drop a bombshell into the middle of this excruciating meal came to her, but she dismissed it. If she announced now to her father that she had no intention of ever agreeing to marry the Count, or anyone else of his choosing, the thing which she dreaded and feared would happen: the King would be furious and humiliated; he'd possibly banish her from Palosia or make sure she stayed here, a virtual prisoner, for ever.

The Count would be free to leave and stop wasting his time on pointless conversation. He might be angry too, she thought, to have his plans to marry her thwarted, whatever his reasons might be for wanting the union to go ahead.

The one thing she was sure of was that he only wanted to marry her for some self-serving reason of his own. She'd been told often enough that nobody else would ever want her. What nobleman or billionaire would be interested in tying himself to a plain girl who wore flat shoes and preferred digging in the garden to shopping or jet-setting?

But, even as she entertained the tempting idea of deliberately sabotaging her own future right here in the elaborate dining room, watched from their portraits on the walls by imperious ancestors, her resolve drained away.

While she felt afraid of her father's rage, it was the idea of how such a scene would upset her mother that caused her to bite her lip and swallow the words that she longed to say. Her gentle mother, who avoided confrontation at all costs and who devoted her life to making a difference to impoverished women and children, would hate to witness such an argument. It would be far better to wait until she could talk to her father in private, when she'd worked out exactly what to say and didn't feel forced into it by the awkwardness of the situation in which she now found herself.

A taut silence settled around the table. Rosabella wondered if her father would break it with a crushing comment, but a glance at him showed his mouth clamped shut and his eyes on the Count. Her coffee cup rattled in the saucer as she picked it up.

'Perhaps Princess Rosabella could show me something of the gardens after lunch?' That voice sent another ripple of…what?…through her and, despite wanting to avoid his eyes, she looked at him again. 'Their reputation is widespread, and I'd be most interested to see them.'

'Very well.' In her peripheral vision Rosabella saw the King nod.

She felt a conflicted gratitude to the Count. He'd smoothly broken the tense silence and turned the attention of the King away from her. But she'd have much preferred it if he'd suggested walking with her father alone. Right now, she longed to escape to her rooms, shed her formal clothes for her comfortable gardening ones and lose herself in a distant corner of the rambling estate where no-one would find her—and especially not the Count, with his missing-nothing eyes.

She'd thought his eyes were dark-grey, almost black. But now she thought they might be the colour of the midnight sky, or that shade of obsidian which was almost blue in its blackness.

Get a grip. The colour of his eyes was of absolutely no interest to her, because after today she'd never have to look into them again or have them study her with that expression of compassionate interest that threatened to make her reconsider all the resolutions she'd made.

CHAPTER FIVE

Rosabella followed her father and the Count down the curved steps that swept from the terrace to the gardens.

As they'd risen from the table, her mother had pleaded a headache and retreated to her quarters. Rosabella wished she could have followed her.

The two men reached the foot of the steps and turned onto the path between the avenue of ancient oaks. In the distance, the marble fountains gleamed. The Count appeared to be deep in conversation with the King and she wondered how he managed to talk with what appeared to be such ease with her father, who was known for his abrupt aloofness, not his conversational skills.

If she turned in the opposite direction and melted away into the terraces of flower beds on the other side of the palace, how long would it be before she was missed? There were numerous arbours covered in roses and jasmine where she could hide.

But, while part of her longed to escape, another

part of her felt pulled towards the Count. He was so completely different from the man she'd expected him to be that she still felt confused. It was as if she'd received a package but, when she opened the box, found it contained something intriguing and exciting instead of the rather dull object she'd anticipated.

The Count's calm confidence unsettled her. It spoke of a man who almost always got what he wanted and would fight for it if challenged. He was here to claim her, and he didn't doubt at all his right to do so. As far as he was concerned, the deed was done. Only the formalities remained to be concluded.

Yet she'd had no say in this marriage. This felt like a story from the past, and not a good one. Hadn't her parents' marriage been brokered in this precise way? She shuddered to think of how her mother had been treated when the possibility of her producing a son had been wiped out by Rosabella's own birth.

When she'd first become aware as a young girl of the turmoil her arrival had caused, she'd been overwhelmed with guilt. How she'd wished things had been different. How much better all their lives would have been if she'd been a boy! When she'd understood that she was the cause of the Queen's inability to have more children, the guilt had intensified. Irrational as it was, that guilt had never left her, and she'd tried to assuage it by being everything her parents could ever have wanted.

It had been a waste of emotion and energy, because the one thing they wanted was the one thing she could never be.

As she watched the interaction between her father and the Count, anger at her situation mounted. Her father appeared to be listening to him intently, and she remembered the futility of the years she'd spent trying to be interesting enough, clever enough or beautiful enough to warrant a glance or a word of praise or encouragement from him.

She was determined that the Count would never see the emotions that seethed beneath her meek exterior. She would be cool towards him. Her composure would not slip again, as it had in those few seconds when she'd realised who he was and she knew he'd read the confusion and longing in her eyes.

The two men paused while her father explained the perspective of the tree-lined walk leading to the focal point of the fountains, and Luca half-turned to look back over his shoulder. He smiled, and it took all her determination to crush her natural instinct to smile back. He moved to one side, creating a gap between himself and her father, and gestured to her to walk between them, but she gave a slight shake of her head.

Rosabella welcomed the shade cast by the trees. When she'd dressed for lunch, hurried and fussed over by Luisa, she hadn't expected to walk in the gardens afterwards and she hadn't brought a hat. The briefest exposure to the August sun could turn her fair skin pink and make the faint sprinkling of tiny freckles across her cheekbones and nose stand out.

The gardens were quiet beneath the blanket of the afternoon heat, as if all living creatures had retreated to the deep shelter of the trees and shady arbours. Normally her father would shut himself in his study with his books at this time of day. Evidently, he was anxious to please or impress his visitor.

The demure high neck and long sleeves of her silk dress felt restrictive, and she longed to be able to feel the air against her skin, even if the breeze was a warm one. Up-to-date, fashionable clothes were readily available in the shops of Palosia, these days, as tourism had increased, but her father insisted that Rosabella dressed conservatively in long sleeves and skirts. Nothing even faintly revealing was permitted.

As they neared the fountains, the cool sound of water splashing from marble conch shells into the surrounding pool made her feel even warmer.

King Fiero slowed his pace. 'I'll rest here.' He indicated a bench beneath the trees. 'Show his Lordship the fountains, Rosabella.'

Rosabella wanted to say that the Count could see the fountains very well without help from her, but she pressed her lips together and nodded. Luca kept a respectful distance from her. He would know that her father had positioned himself where he could keep an eye on them, and he would be sure to observe decorum.

The view was spectacular. Beyond the fountains, the gardens fell away towards the valley, the terraces becoming increasingly wild until they merged with the woodland below. Further away, the mountains thrust jagged peaks of rock into the bleached sky. Luca imagined that in winter, snow would soften their outlines and lend a bite to the wind that whistled across the island.

From what he'd seen, Palosia was a perfect universe all of its own. There were towering mountains, verdant valleys, clear rivers and streams and beaches of fine, white sand. The azure Mediterranean encircled it all, isolating it, yet also linking it with other nearby islands, and the mainland of Europe was not too great a distance away to the north. Luca didn't think he'd ever been anywhere which more closely resembled his idea of paradise.

He turned towards Rosabella and swept an arm in an arc, encompassing the vista.

'I've always thought Tuscany beautiful, but this...' He shook his head. 'This is more dramatic, more varied, more...unique.'

Was this the reason why she was cold towards him? Did she dread being taken from her home and forced to live somewhere new and alien? Perhaps she'd be relieved when he announced he was cancelling their engagement.

If that was so, then he should feel pleased about what he planned to do. Why, then, did something make him feel the tiniest bit of regret that he would not be marrying her and making her his?

He dismissed the thought. He'd been seduced by the sumptuous palace, the glorious gardens and the attention that King Fiero had paid him, nothing more. The castle in Tuscany, which was now his, was known as one of the grandest in Italy, with its Renaissance frescoes, marble statuary and flourishing vineyards that produced some of the most famous Italian wines.

He wanted for nothing and yet here, on Palosia, he felt that something in his life was lacking. It was because he'd just wrapped up that difficult case in New York and had not yet had the opportunity to start on the next one, he told himself. His life consisted of moving from one challenging brief to another. That was how he liked it.

The sudden death of his father had been shocking, but he would have dealt with it with swift efficiency if the startling matter of his engagement to a princess had not come to light. Knowing that his father had kept this secret from him, waiting to spring it on him when he saw fit, infuriated him. All the measures he'd taken over the years to escape and build his own successful life, had been futile. His father had held the trump card all along.

Well, it was a pity the old man hadn't stayed alive long enough to see that he would never agree to this archaic and ridiculous arrangement. Just as his father had failed to control his wife, he'd fail to control his son. If he hadn't forbidden his mother to ride that untamed horse, she wouldn't have felt the need to defy him. Luca imagined how his mother must have chafed against the constant restrictions her husband had imposed on her, and how her frustration had finally made her do something so wild and dangerous that she'd paid for it with her life.

People said Luca had inherited his free spirit and determination to be independent from her. Looking back, he supposed he'd been a constant reminder to his father of how he'd failed to mould his young wife to the shape he wanted. Agreeing to marry Luca to a woman of his choosing must have felt like a way of keeping him in line.

He'd be kind and considerate to Princess Rosabella, but agree to *marry* her? Never. It was his father's attempt to force him into obedience and that made it the last thing in the world he would do.

Luca dragged his eyes from the stunning view in time to see Princess Rosabella quickly avert her gaze from him. His expression was probably grim, reflecting his thoughts, and he dipped his head, trying to find a smile to give her to defuse the tension that crackled between them in the warm air.

The heat felt suffocating. He slid his jacket off his shoulders and spread it on the marble seat that encircled the fountain.

'Shall we rest here for a few minutes? The outlook is magnificent.'

He watched as her conflicted expression gave way to one of acceptance, and she nodded and sat down carefully on his jacket after a quick glance in the direction of her father. The marble figures of the fountain blocked the King's view of them. Was that why she'd agreed to sit with him?

Her spine was straight and stiff. As he sat down near her, she kept her eyes fixed on the distant mountains rather than turning her head to meet his. Her flushed cheeks made him think her silk dress was much too warm. The slight tilt of her nose, her fine jawline and her luminous dark-chocolate eyes stirred something in him. Then his memory landed on an angel on one of the frescoes in the castle in Tuscany. If her hair could be freed from its restraining pearls and pins and allowed to float down her back in its natural waves... Luca was surprised to find that he wanted to liberate it himself.

'How long will you be staying?'

The question surprised him. Was this her attempt at polite conversation, or was she genuinely interested? If so, he wondered what she hoped to hear.

'I'll return to Italy tomorrow morning.' Although, after his meeting with King Fiero later this afternoon, he might have to leave tonight.

'Oh! So soon? I thought...'

Her stiff formality slipped for an instant, but only an instant, and it was impossible to tell whether that was relief in her voice or disappointment. What could he say that might make her relax enough to deliver another one of the smiles she'd given him when she'd walked away from him earlier?

'If there were fish in this fountain, would you sing to them?'

There was a flash of surprise in her eyes as she turned her head towards him.

'There are no fish in this fountain, so...' She lifted her shoulders and dropped them again, then glanced up at the cupids and their conch shells endlessly splashing water into the marble basin. Whatever she'd expected him to say, it hadn't been that.

'I said "if". Would you?'

'I've grown out of that. It was a long time ago.'

'Even if I asked you to sing?'

'Especially if you asked me to sing.'

He watched her dark lashes sweep to her cheeks. The bones of her knuckles gleamed white as she gripped the edge of the seat, supporting her rigid, upright posture.

'Why is that? It was so joyful and carefree.'

Finally, she lifted her gaze to his face. 'Perhaps at the age of four I was joyful and carefree, Count Montenale. But, as I said, I've grown up.'

'And grown out of joyfulness? Yet when I saw you earlier you seemed closer to that child than you do now.'

'That was before I... Before we...'

The sideways glance she sent him from under her lashes was quick, and she shook her head.

'That was when I still thought you were a gardener and you thought I was...who?'

She released her grip on the edge of the bench and twisted her fingers together in her lap.

'I don't know. Perhaps just another envoy come to petition the King for something. I never thought that...'

'That the person you crashed into might be your future husband?'

He heard her sharp intake of breath. 'No, I never thought that. You were...you are...'

He waited but she was silent, staring down at her interlaced fingers.

'I'm what?' he prompted.

'You're just not what I expected.' When she eventually spoke, her words came in a rush.

Luca leaned forward, resting his folded arms on his knees. He kept his eyes on the distant mountains, feeling she was more likely to engage with him if they didn't make eye contact.

'Then what...or *who*...were you expecting?' He felt intrigued and a little mystified. 'You did know I was coming?'

Her teeth worried her bottom lip and a faint frown creased the space between her brows.

'Yes. And I...don't know. I just wasn't expecting someone like you.'

'What am I like?'

'Do you always ask so many questions?'

He turned his head to look at her then. 'I'm a lawyer, Princess Rosabella. Asking questions is what I do most of the time.'

Her startled eyes flew to his.

'A *lawyer*? But... I thought you were an Italian count.'

'The two are not mutually exclusive.' He

smiled. 'I know because I'm both. Except I'm still testing out the "count" bit.' He saw the question in her eyes. 'My father passed away recently. I've inherited his title, so I am the *new* count. It still feels strange.'

'I'm sorry. When...?' There was compassion in her voice.

Luca shook his head. 'Perhaps that's a story for another time. But how come you don't know more about me? After all, we've been engaged for twenty years. Have you looked me up on the Internet?'

It occurred to him, for the first time, that she might not have access to the Internet, unbelievable as that seemed. There was Internet on Palosia, but she appeared to be so protected, so unworldly...so controlled by her father.

Unease stirred in his gut. He'd had to fight that particular kind of control. It had been a lifelong struggle to hold onto his determination and self-belief. For a young woman isolated in this palace, it would have been very difficult.

He saw her emotions shut down again. The hint of compassion that had sparked in the dark depths of her eyes was wiped out and her expression reverted to one of cool indifference. She turned away from him, her chin lifted.

'Until my father introduced us, I didn't even know your name.'

Shock took him by surprise, momentarily shredding his careful composure.

'What?'

She rose quickly. 'I need to go. The sun is too hot, and I don't have a hat.'

'Of course.' Luca was on his feet in an instant, his good manners restored, but his thoughts were in turmoil, trying to play catch-up, although nothing made proper sense. He didn't like that. His lawyer's brain needed facts to be clear and logical. Mysteries needed to be explained as quickly and efficiently as possible. Surprises were unwelcome because they meant he'd failed to anticipate something important. 'Surely your father…?'

He knew she was telling the truth. There was something in her gaze and her manner that spoke of simple honesty. He was good at recognising that when he saw it.

Why had her father hidden the identity of her proposed husband from her? Having briefly observed King Fiero's dismissive behaviour towards his wife and daughter, he thought he knew the answer. Queen Chiara and Princess Rosabella were unimportant women who didn't need to be kept informed about what he had planned for them, and he obviously had no expectation that they wouldn't always obey him.

Now he heard King Fiero's authoritarian voice summoning them. Uncertainty flickered across the princess's face and then anxiety quickly replaced her look of cold distance.

Without thinking, needing to reassure her, he put a hand on her arm. Her attention, twisted towards her father, slowly turned back and she appeared to freeze as her eyes fixed on his fingers where they lay across her forearm. Then her shocked gaze lifted to lock with his.

'It's okay.' He kept his voice even and soft, but the sound of it seemed to jolt her into action.

She snatched her arm from under his hand, folding her arms tightly across her body and shaking her head. 'No! It's...not. At least, it won't be okay if I don't answer him at once.'

'I apologise. I'm truly sorry. I only meant to reassure you, not to offend you.'

Colour that he was sure had nothing to do with exposure to the sun stained her pale cheeks and she dropped her gaze, shaking her head again.

'I'm...not offended. But...'

The King's voice came again, calling her name. Luca watched her inhale a deep, shaky breath, and then she walked away from him, out of the bright sunlight and into the shade. He had the strangest feeling that somewhere in the vicinity a light had been extinguished.

He picked up his jacket and shrugged it on, straightening his shirt cuffs and doing up one button, keeping his eyes on Princess Rosabella.

He watched as she stopped in front of her father and heard him bark a question at her. He could see her shake her head from where he stood. King Fiero's eyes sought him out, boring into him as he walked towards him.

Luca refused to quicken his pace, or apologise to this man for keeping him waiting. Mostly what he wanted to do was to tell him, right here and now, that he could shred the document that he'd drawn up twenty years ago with his own treacherous father because he would never, ever consent to a marriage of convenience, and that he'd be leaving Palosia as soon as possible.

But long experience made him breathe in and pause. Acting on impulse was never advisable. While he wanted to bring this unfortunate episode in his life to a quick conclusion, as he watched the princess walk away from him he felt an unwelcome need to find out more about her. If he left now, in anger, what repercussions would that have for her and her future?

And did it really concern him? The aim of this visit to Palosia was to extricate himself from the agreement their two fathers had drawn up, not to involve himself in the life of the princess he had no intention of marrying.

But before he could leave he would have to make sure that no harm would come to her because of his actions. In his profession, he gave a voice to those who had none; should he be willing to speak for Princess Rosabella, who no longer had a voice to sing to the fish about pretty horses?

He needed to take a step back and focus on what he'd come here to do. Morally, he felt bound to tell King Fiero immediately that he was not going to marry Princess Rosabella, but as soon as he'd done that he'd no longer be welcome on Palosia. He'd have to leave immediately. Anything other than his swift extrication from the agreement could lead to him becoming entangled in the affairs of this family and giving his father a voice in the way he lived his life.

So why did he feel a burden of responsibility for the princess's welfare? As he watched her walk away, the thought hit him that he might never see her again. A shaft of regret stabbed him somewhere in the region of his heart, but he made up his mind to ignore it.

CHAPTER SIX

When the first pale fingers of light crept around the edges of the heavy curtains at the windows, Rosabella gave up all hope of sleep.

She kicked off the bed covers, slid to the floor and padded across the thick carpet to the window, pulling back the drapes. The valley below the palace was shrouded in mist but the sky above the mountains was streaked with gold and pink, promising another warm day, just like yesterday.

Only no other day would ever be like yesterday. Reliving it in every detail had kept her fitfully awake through the dark hours of the night. That, and the knowledge that *he* was sleeping somewhere in the palace.

Colliding headlong with the stranger, and that fleeting sense of being *protected* as his hands had stopped her from falling, then the shock that had threatened to immobilise her when she'd discovered his identity, had played in her mind on repeat. She'd thought over and over again of the moment when their eyes had met as he'd bowed over her hand, and all her convictions about the evils of a marriage of convenience had seemed to tremble, on the brink of collapse.

With no facts to go on before now, it had been left to her imagination to conjure up an image of the man who was willing to marry the graceless, plain, frankly unladylike person she was. He'd be older, austere and dismissive of her, interested only in the prestige that marrying into an ancient royal family could bring him. And he'd expect her to produce an heir, and spare, in rapid succession.

Then he'd leave her in some remote wing of his castle, thinking she should be grateful to him for rescuing her from a lonely, single life. That was how her parents' marriage had played out, and she had no other example with which to compare it.

If the Count had been anything like the man she'd imagined, it would have been easier to remain steadfast in the face of her father's anticipated anger.

But he wasn't. Not at all. His manner had been warm, his actions considerate and he seemed to have a genuine interest in her. If his presence on Palosia was merely to finalise the details of their marriage, he'd hidden the business side of his visit well.

His calm gaze seemed to see into her soul and

understand her thoughts. She could get terrifyingly lost in those dark eyes, but losing herself with him wouldn't be frightening because he made her feel...*safe*. The way a corner of his mouth tipped up a fraction when he was amused did something unfamiliar and strange to her insides. With her eyes caught in his, she'd had the unsettling thought that she could give up all her idealism about marrying for everlasting love in a heartbeat if she could marry this man.

If being his wife would mean feeling the warmth of that searching gaze resting on her face, and the reassuring touch of his hands on her arms again, she wouldn't care if it was merely a marriage of convenience. Perhaps, sometime in the future, she'd be able to persuade him to change his attitude to her; to see her in a different light...

The insanity of her thoughts had lasted seconds. She'd pulled herself back to the reality of meeting the man who wanted to marry her for his own materialistic reasons. His sincerity had to be a mask, his warmth and interest fake. How could it be anything else, when he'd only just met her?

Besides, she knew very well that no man would ever want to be with her for *herself*. She'd been taught that from an early age.

She thought of her sister and the joy she'd found in marrying the man she loved, and who loved her back without reservation or condition. She remembered the humiliation and misery her mother continued to endure for failing to match up to her father's demands. If she couldn't marry for love like Sofia had done, she'd never marry at all. And since even her own father could not love or even tolerate her, no other man ever would, obviously.

Until the Count had laid his hand on her arm, it had been fine, she told herself. Her determination to maintain an icy demeanour had held firm after that first meeting, and following the few minutes they'd spent together at the fountain she'd been within seconds of excusing herself from his presence. The touch of his fingers on her forearm, even through the barrier of her silk sleeve, had changed that.

Rosabella turned her back on the glory of the early morning revealing itself beneath her window and paced across her bedroom floor. She stopped in front of the full-length mirror, in its elaborate gold frame that hung on the wall.

It would be perfectly obvious to anyone who chose to study her closely this morning that she'd had a restless, largely sleepless night. Her fair hair, which had been pulled into a sleek knot yesterday, flowed over her shoulders and down her back in a tangle of curls. Rubbing her eyes had made them red and there were dark smudges beneath them.

Growing stronger by the minute, light gleamed through the windows behind her, illuminating her body through her translucent cotton nightgown. She studied her curves and planes, trying and failing to imagine how anyone could ever find her attractive. Her legs were too long and her breasts too small. While there was an acceptable curve at her waist, her hips could never be described as 'childbearing', and surely that was what any husband would require?

The convenience part of a brokered marriage would mean the swift arrival of children, preferably at least one boy. And if she failed to provide those essential commodities…well, she'd have failed as a wife and a woman. She only had to look to her mother to see what would happen next.

Then her fingers strayed to the place on her arm where Luca's hand had rested until she'd recoiled in shock. The cause of the shock was the fact that he'd touched her. The way it had affected her had made her freeze, her eyes scanning his face to see if he was experiencing something similar.

When she'd reached the sanctuary of her room yesterday afternoon, she'd tugged the silk dress over her head, sending hairpins and pearl clips flying in all directions, and studied her arm. She'd felt almost disappointed not to see the marks of his fingers branded on her skin. Her heartbeat and ragged breathing had taken long minutes to return to something like normal, although she'd told herself that her breathless, flustered state was the result of walking too quickly in the heat.

His touch had only lasted seconds, but a pulse of energy had travelled up her arm and down into the pit of her stomach, triggering an intense tightening, hollowing sensation that had alarmed her. Yet she longed to feel it again.

He'd be leaving this morning. Rosabella ran her fingers over the skin of her forearm and then pressed her palms flat against her abdomen. Once she'd confronted her father, would she be ready to accept that she'd never see the Count again? Would he be angry? Or would he shrug her off as forgettable, and find some other royal bride who would willingly marry him and do his bidding?

The thought caused a strange tightness around her heart. If she could have just one more chance to experience those strange, electrifying sensations he'd stirred in her, she knew she'd seize it.

Even though she'd longed to be able to change back into her gardening clothes yesterday afternoon and lose herself in the terraces, when she'd reached her room she'd felt too wrung out and confused to want to leave it again.

She'd tried to read but the words on the page kept blurring as her mind returned to Luca. She'd made a huge effort to be rational. He'd only touched her to reassure her, and he could have no idea of how that had made her feel. If he had, he'd have found her reaction amusing. A corner of his mouth would have quirked in the way that sent a tingle up her spine...

There seemed to be no escape from her thoughts. She'd asked Luisa to bring some soup to her room but she hadn't even been able to eat that.

Now, frustrated, she pushed her hands into her hair and pressed her palms against her temples. Enough! Much more of this and all her resolutions would crumble to dust. The Count had not asked to see her again after she'd walked away from him, and for all she knew he was already back in Tuscany. She'd put him out of her mind before these endless thoughts drove her to distraction.

Today she'd request a meeting with her father and tell him she wouldn't be marrying anyone. In the meantime, she'd take herself to one of the furthest corners of the garden so that she wouldn't have to see or speak to another soul for hours. Gardening would calm her mind and allow her time to think and plan. Although she'd already decided what she would say to her father, she could spend the morning perfecting her speech and preparing answers to the questions he was bound to fling at her.

Luisa had stuffed her dusty linen skirt and smock into the laundry basket but Rosabella pulled them out and put them on again, relishing the comfort of the worn fabric compared with the expensive silk she'd had to wear yesterday.

Opening the tall windows that led onto a narrow balcony, she took her hairbrush and a ribbon out into the early-morning sunshine and sat down at the little table from where the view stretched all the way to a glimpse of the distant sea.

She pulled up her feet, sat cross-legged on the chair and began the slow task of teasing the knots out of her hair. When it was finally tangle-free, she brushed it, finding the long, slow strokes soothing.

As her nimble fingers wove the final strands of her braid and tied the ribbon around the end, there was a knock on her bedroom door. Luisa swept in with a swish of her skirts and the crackle of her starched apron and Rosabella could tell at once that she was bringing more than just the coffee and fruit she had for breakfast every morning. She deposited the tray on the table in front of Rosabella and planted her fists on her hips, shaking her head.

'Thank you, Luisa, but I can see you want to tell me something. What's wrong?'

'It's your clothes, Princess Rosabella.' The disparaging look she cast over her matched the tone of her voice. 'They will not do.'

Rosabella conjured up a smile, surprised that she was able to, considering the way she'd been tormented in the night by thoughts of the Count, and was now mentally trembling at the prospect of the meeting she anticipated having with her father.

'They're perfectly fine for what I'm planning to do in the garden this morning.'

'But I put them in the laundry basket. They need washing.'

'And I took them out. There's no point in washing clothes which I'll only get dirty again.'

Luisa sighed. 'After you marry the Count, you'll have no use for them.' She waved a hand dismissively. 'You'll have gardeners to do all that work. You'll wear beautiful dresses and polish on your nails and…behave like a princess.'

Rosabella drew in a breath to tell Luisa that her fantasy was doomed but remembered in time that she had to keep her decision a secret until she'd revealed her intentions to her father.

Instead, she shook her head. 'Well, there're

gardeners here to do the work, yet I enjoy doing it myself. And since my marriage to the Count has not happened yet, I can spend today in the garden.'

She poured coffee into the delicate cup, inhaling its rich aroma. She studied Luisa over the porcelain rim. 'But commenting on my clothes was not what you were going to do when you came in.' She swallowed a mouthful of the dark, hot liquid and sighed. 'Perfect coffee, thank you. Now, what was it you were going to say?'

Luisa folded her arms. 'I wish I had come in a little earlier. I could have saved you the trouble.' She indicated the smooth braid that lay over Rosabella's shoulder. 'I will have to undo that braid and put your hair up again.'

Rosabella laughed. 'Since when did a gardener need a fancy hairstyle?'

'Ah, this morning you may admire the gardens, but you will not be doing any digging or getting your hands dirty. You will be going for a walk with the Count.'

Shock made Rosabella gasp. She choked on a mouthful of coffee, spilling some of it over her linen smock. The hot liquid trickled down her front, soaking through the fabric.

'The *Count*?' The cup rattled against the saucer as she replaced it. 'But…he's gone. Or, he's going this morning.'

Luisa unfolded the damask napkin from the tray and used it to mop at Rosabella's top. 'This is hot, Princess Rosabella. I hope it didn't burn you.'

Rosabella plucked at the soaked fabric, pulling it away from her skin. It was hot, but she hadn't noticed. She pulled up her knees and wrapped her arms around them, gripping her fingers together to hide their shaking.

'No, you must be mistaken, Luisa. Yesterday we walked in the garden, through the oak avenue to the marble fountain, where we sat for a while. The Count...well, he said clearly that he would be leaving this morning.'

She swallowed, aware that she was talking too much, but wanting to relive the moments at the fountain. She bit her bottom lip.

'Leaving? Today?' Luisa shook her head and waved a hand in a dismissive gesture. 'Of course not. He will want to get to know you a little, so we must go and choose a dress for you to wear, and do your hair again, so that he will see you at your best.'

'But he *said*...'

'Perhaps you misheard or misunderstood. It was very hot yesterday and you were upset and flustered when you returned to your room—a touch of the sun, perhaps.' She leaned forward and looked closely at Rosabella's face. 'Mmm, those freckles...'

Rosabella unlinked her hands and wiped her palms over her face, as if she might be able to rub out the offending freckles. Then she stopped and turned her face towards the morning sun.

'What if I happen to like my freckles? I won't try to hide them.'

'Very well, but eat some fruit. You will need energy for your walk. The grapes are delicious.'

Rosabella eyed the bowl of fruit but did not feel tempted.

'Who,' she asked, suddenly suspicious, 'Told you that the Count was staying longer than he'd planned and would like to walk with me? Because, if it was my father, it might simply be what he *expects*.'

'It was Paulo. When he served the Count his breakfast, he was specifically requested to send a message to you. He told Paulo he would be staying for perhaps a week.'

'A *week*?'

CHAPTER SEVEN

Luca stood on the gravel path, just beyond the archway, a few steps from where Princess Rosabella had crashed into him the previous day.

A breeze ruffled his hair, but the sun was already warm on his back and he knew the temperature would climb quickly towards noon. But for now the day was perfect, with crystalline air and a matchless blue sky. The distant sound of voices floated up to him from the village far below, and somewhere he heard a church clock begin to strike. He counted the chimes to ten.

Ten o'clock was the agreed time for his meeting with Princess Rosabella. He had been here for five minutes already and, although he told himself that to be late would have been impolite, he knew the truth was that he was impatient to see her again. He pushed his hands into the pockets of his jeans, determined not to check his watch. To be seen doing that would also be considered impolite.

But as the minutes ticked by doubt began to

niggle at him. What if she didn't show up? She'd been shocked when he'd touched her arm yesterday and, although he'd apologised at once, she'd walked away without looking back. Perhaps what he'd taken for shock had been annoyance or dislike. There'd seemed to be some confusion when he'd enquired about her later, but eventually the Queen's lady-in-waiting had sent a message to say Princess Rosabella was indisposed. The warm day had been too much for her delicate constitution.

Luca had frowned at that information. What did 'indisposed' actually mean? Was she ill? Or did she simply not wish to see him? Also, Princess Rosabella did not seem delicate to him. He'd felt the wiry strength in her upper arms when he'd steadied her and had secretly admired her upright posture and firm step as they'd walked through the avenue of oaks.

It had been the sight of her straight and determined back that had made him change his mind about leaving Palosia so abruptly. Although she seemed determined to project an image of strength, he suspected there was something much more complex going on beneath the surface.

She'd been shocked by his touch, yes, but after her initial confusion she'd tried to cover it up. That she'd had to try meant she was determined not to let him know he'd stirred any feelings in her, but he strongly suspected that he had. She'd frozen, and he'd seen the confusion in her eyes when she'd dragged them away from his hand to meet his gaze, and, if he was not mistaken, he'd also seen a want or need for something that went deep. He wondered if she had any understanding of her reaction and what it had communicated to him.

When had the simple touch of his fingers ever elicited such a marked response from a woman? Stupid question, he told himself, because the answer was 'never'. He thought about the last woman he'd dated. She'd been a finance executive, with a head for numbers and a body honed and toned to perfection by hours with a personal trainer and a dedication to avoiding carbs. Her response to him had been cool over dinner, and then clinically controlled later in his bed.

The episode had left him feeling dissatisfied on every level, but he'd realised that, in the life he lived, he'd come to expect nothing more. The memory of the sudden bright flash of sensation he'd felt when he'd held the princess upright was more vibrant than any other encounter he could remember. The recognition seemed to link them when their eyes had locked over their hands in the King's antechamber had made him feel curiously charged.

There was nothing to compare between those

brief moments and his most recent cold and mechanical date in New York. Was it simply because Princess Rosabella was inexperienced with men? Or was it her natural spontaneity that came across to him as fresh and unspoilt? Whatever it was, her response intrigued him.

The King had been surprised when he'd said he'd like to stay for a few days so that he and the princess could become better acquainted. Without saying as much, he'd given Luca the impression that he felt it an unnecessary waste of time—as if to say, what difference would it make, once they were married, whether they knew each other or not? But he'd shrugged his shoulders and agreed, and also stipulated that Luca and Rosabella could spend time together on condition that they were supervised by a chaperone.

Luca mused that he could have taken offence at the inference that he was not to be trusted alone with the princess but had decided it was not worth the trouble it might cause. His intention was not to seduce her but to make sure that when he announced he was not marrying her she would not be blamed. He would use their time together to explain gently the reasons why he could not stand by the marriage agreement. She would be perfectly safe with him.

Impatience got the better of him and he pulled

a hand from his pocket and glanced at his watch. Ten minutes had passed since he'd heard the church clock in the valley, and...

There was the sound of a light step on the gravel behind him and he turned.

She trod carefully across the courtyard, hearing only the faintest click of the French windows as her chaperone closed the door—grimly resentful at being made to trail around after the count and the princess for the morning, if her frown was anything to go by.

She stepped around the corner into the archway, still hidden by deep shade, and stopped in her tracks. All the imaginings that had plagued her during the night immediately faded into insignificance. He was *more*...so much *more*...than the image her mind had preserved, even though all she could see of him was his back.

Slim black jeans, slung low on his hips, accentuated the length of his legs and the power of his thighs. When had anyone ever worn *jeans* in the palace of Palosia? A narrow tan leather belt was threaded through the loops. A pale-grey cotton shirt with a fine white stripe did nothing to disguise the width of his shoulders and she could see that he'd rolled the sleeves up to the elbows. Thick, dark hair curled slightly at his nape, and the sight of it did odd things to her fingers, making them want to feel if it was as thick and soft as it looked. His hands were pushed into his pockets and she quickly buried her own in the deep pockets of her dress in case they ignored her silent pleas to behave.

What was happening to her? When had she ever had this powerful urge to touch someone who was virtually a stranger, and definitely a man from whom she must keep a cool distance?

If she could make him not want to marry her, the future would be so much easier. It would mean she could avoid the confrontation with her father which she knew was going to rip a hole in the fabric of her life. So, formal and polite, but cold, was how she should be. Wasn't it?

But how could she be unmoved and cool when her heart had leapt into overdrive, hammering against her ribs, and a warm tide of something she did not recognise flooded her whole being, making her knees feel stupidly weak?

As she watched, he pulled his left hand from his pocket and she caught a glimpse of a strong forearm and the flash of a gold watch as he bent his head to check the time. She knew she was late, but she'd have been later still if she'd given in and allowed Luisa to undo her braid and perform a gravity-defying miracle with her hair.

Sharp fingers belonging to the chaperone nudged her in the small of her back and gave her a little push towards the sunlight. 'Go on. Greet him,' her voice hissed in Rosabella's ear.

Her sandals crunched on the gravel as she stepped forward, and he turned. The view of his broad back and long, powerful legs had not prepared her at all. The top two buttons of the grey shirt were undone and Rosabella's eyes fixed, mesmerised, on the smooth tanned skin of his throat, neck and the hint of dark hair that showed below it. Somehow remembering it was rude to stare, she dragged her gaze upward and felt the warmth of those calm, all-seeing dark eyes land on her face. His hair had a mussed look, as if he'd raked his fingers through it, and some of it flopped forward over his forehead.

Quite simply, she stole his breath away.

She wore a wide-brimmed straw hat that cast her face in shadow, but her luminous brown eyes, fringed with long lashes, shone from beneath the brim. They rose from where she appeared to be staring at his chest and met his own.

Her sunshine-yellow linen dress with heart-shaped neckline hugged the slight curves of her body but fell in soft pleats from her slim hips to her calves. Three-quarter length sleeves ended in buttoned cuffs. She stood a little way from him and it looked as if her feet, in bronze leather sandals, were ready to turn and run at a second's notice; she was as unsure and jumpy as a startled fawn.

His first instinct was to put out a hand to stop her from fleeing, but that hadn't gone well yesterday. Calling on a store of control he normally reserved for difficult moments in the courtroom, he kept his arms at his sides. The last thing he wanted was to scare her off before they'd exchanged a single word.

'Good morning, Princess Rosabella. What a beautiful day for a walk in these glorious gardens.'

A faint flush stained her cheeks. Her mouth opened, feather-soft beneath a slick of balm, and the tip of her tongue touched her bottom lip. Luca felt a punch of reaction so strong that he feared he had visibly flinched.

Small earrings in the shape of daisies fashioned from crystal shone at her earlobes. He was irrationally pleased to see that she wore her hair in the long braid he'd first seen the previous day. A pale-gold silk ribbon secured the end of it. Her hands were buried in the deep pockets of the pleats of her dress.

She nodded and he found himself entranced by how her earrings sparkled. 'The gardens are beautiful in all weathers and seasons.' She drew a hand from a pocket and touched the bow that tied her plait, drawing his eyes to her slender fingers. An image of them entwined with his own danced in his imagination.

'Your hair...' Luca bit his lip. He'd only have himself to blame if she was offended or frightened away by this personal comment, but the words had escaped in response to the fascination her hair held for him. At lunch yesterday he'd spent some time wondering how that amount of lustrous hair had been tamed and confined into the pleat resting at the nape of her neck. The thoughts had distracted him from his conversation with the King and then he had castigated himself for allowing them at all. He was here to extract himself from a frankly mediaeval agreement which sought to bind him to this girl for ever, not to fantasize about her hair.

That little frown he'd seen yesterday creased her forehead and she looked stricken. 'Oh!' She flicked the thick rope of the braid over her shoulder. 'Luisa wanted to put it up but there wasn't time...'

'No,' he said quickly. 'I mean, I like it like that. It's beautiful. It's a pity to hide it in a formal style.'

Her lips curved in a slight smile, and he remembered the promise of a dimple in her left cheek.

'Thank you. But I don't believe this can be an informal walk, in spite of my hair style.'

'Oh, I think it can. Although...' He glanced behind her to the figure of a woman in the shadow of the arch.

She dipped her head. 'My chaperone will make sure it's kept formal enough. Did you request her, or was she my father's idea?'

'It wasn't mine, but your father expressed surprise that I might want to get to know you, even though he intends for you to marry me.'

'No, he wouldn't see the point. After all, surely there'd be enough time afterwards to make my acquaintance? Perhaps he thinks if you find out too much about me beforehand you might change your mind.'

He looked for a sign that she was teasing him but found none. Her gaze was steady and serious.

'Surely he would want you, his daughter, to get to know her proposed husband a little too?'

She dropped her eyes and shook her head. 'No. In his opinion, that would be an even greater waste of time.'

Regret stabbed at him as he thought about what he intended to do. Would he shatter all this girl's precious dreams of marriage and freedom from the seeming tyranny of her uncaring parent when he abandoned the agreement their fathers had struck? What kind of future would he condemn her to?

But then he remembered why he had to do it.

The shock of discovering what his father had done, plotting and dictating how he should lead his life, would burn for ever. Had he honestly believed that he could force his son to go through with it?

Anger strengthened his resolve. His mother had fought against the iron bonds her husband had forced on her, and her rebellious reaction had killed her. As an adult, he'd wondered if she'd been given the choice between living the rest of her life under the relentless and stultifying control of her husband, or dying on a wild, exhilarating last gallop, which she would have chosen.

After his mother's death he'd been sent to live with her elderly parents. They had raised him in a home filled with love and gentle kindness, teaching him to care for those less fortunate than himself and always to consider the feelings of others. But on his tenth birthday his father had demanded his return. He'd stood in his father's study, confused and afraid before this man who was virtually a stranger, to be told that his real education was about to begin and from then on he would do his bidding and no-one else's.

But the principles his grandparents had instilled in him had prevailed and his own fight for independence had begun that day, alongside the education his father had deemed fit for his heir. It had been a long and bitter battle, culminating in the estrangement of father and son.

There was no way, ever, that he'd give up what he'd fought so hard for and go ahead with the marriage his father had tried to bind him to. To do that would feel like surrendering his soul.

Mentally, he shrugged off her words with a smile. He pushed a hand through his hair and shook his head. The question he'd seen in her eyes when she'd raised them again had died, and he thought she had possibly hoped he would vehemently deny what she'd suggested.

The code of scrupulous honesty by which he lived bound him to speak the truth, so he said nothing. Better to remain silent than to voice his growing dislike of her father. He glanced over at the woman who had been instructed to protect the princess's honour. She had most likely been told to report back any conversation they had to the King.

So he half-turned away from Rosabella, his eyes sweeping over the distant view and the nearer terraces of the gardens.

'I suggested ten o'clock as I thought we could explore the gardens before it grows too warm. I hope this isn't too early for you. I understand you suffered from the effects of the heat yesterday.'

'Oh! Yes, I... It was very warm.' She dropped her gaze. 'Thank you for your consideration.'

'And you had neglected to bring a hat for protection.' He glanced at the intricately woven straw hat she wore. 'I'll ask you to lead the way, princess, since you have a lifelong knowledge of the gardens.'

'If we're to stop walking before it becomes uncomfortably warm, we'll only see a small part of them.'

'I believe the weather on Palosia is reliably settled at this time of year, so perhaps tomorrow we can explore further? That is, if I'll not be taking you away from any official duties.'

'It could always be arranged for the head gardener to show you around, if necessary.'

'Surely that would defeat my purpose?' He kept his voice gentle. 'After all, it is you I wish to know, not the head gardener, even though I'm sure his knowledge is faultless.'

Without replying, Rosabella turned on her heel. 'If we take this path, we can follow a circuit around the flower garden and through the orchard terraces.'

Luca fell in beside her, leaving enough space between them to placate their chaperone. Her delicate floral scent was unlike any of the perfumes with which he was familiar. It had a lightness and freshness which its elusiveness somehow made alluring. He wanted to ask her about it but decided to steer clear of a question that she might find too personal. He didn't want to jeopardise any chance he had of getting her to relax a little in his company.

He realised that what he desired most from the morning was to spend the next two hours with her, and he was determined not to do or say anything at all that might frighten her away or upset her. He wanted to know more about her, listen to her soft voice telling him about the plants and flowers and ask her what had led her to sing to the fish—and what had made her stop.

If he was still here in a few days, perhaps they'd have reached a level of familiarity with each other that would allow him to comment on her perfume.

He put a brake on his thoughts. They could never become familiar with one another. He needed to banish from his mind that image of their intertwined fingers. It was unlikely he'd still need to be here in a few days. With his honed skills of communication and negotiation, he'd tell her why he couldn't marry her, and then tell King Fiero too.

He'd accomplish what he needed to do in less than a few days and be gone.

Walking with the Count at her side made Rosabella self-conscious. The distance between them felt charged with something like magnetism, and she held herself stiffly to resist the invisible force that tugged her closer to him.

What reason could he have for wanting to get to know her better? It was absolutely unnecessary, although it demonstrated a concern for her feelings which she thought was kind.

The repellent image of the man she'd expected to meet was fading rapidly from her memory in the presence of Count Luca. His consideration confused her, and she thought again of how her determination had wavered in the aftermath of the tangle of emotions that had assaulted her when he'd touched her, and how she'd longed to feel that jolt of electricity and that curious warm, melting sensation in her stomach again.

But that had been during the long night when her thoughts had become a jumble of wants and forbidden desires which she didn't understand or recognise. It was much easier to be rational and reasonable in the bright morning sunlight.

She could be herself in the gardens, without reservation or pretence. She knew every inch of the land, including the secluded places cooled by trickling rills of clear water and shaded by giant tree ferns, where she could escape from the heat of the sun and the eyes of the palace staff. She had no intention of showing any of those places to the Count.

But, instead of feeling the sense of calm and

peace which she always found among the flowers and trees, she felt like an exhibit, or a tour guide—as if he would use this time to judge her and, naturally, find her wanting in all the areas which he'd think were important.

She lacked the skill in making polite small-talk and wouldn't know how to begin to attract the interest of a man. Those were social skills that she'd never been taught. Since her future had been determined from the age of four, it had been deemed unnecessary for her to learn them. And now she had no interest in acquiring them. After all, what use would they be to someone who intended to spend the rest of her life tending these beautiful acres?

Besides, she knew she was plain. She had freckles that came out with the sun, and wild hair which had to be tamed in a braid or a complicated knot, held in place with sharp hair pins.

When Count Luca discovered her lack of grace, coupled with the lack of beauty which he would already have noticed, perhaps he'd stop trying to get to know her and go home to his castle in Tuscany. He'd been kind to say he liked her hair, but for all she knew that was a standard compliment that men paid to women. To everyone else, her hair had only ever been a source of irritation.

If he really did intend to remain for several

days, she would have to delay telling her father that she would not marry him. While he was here, staying in the palace, her father would never take any notice of what she said. In fact, if her father thought she was going to embarrass him and cause an unpleasant scene, he might insist that the marriage take place immediately. A prickle of apprehension ran down her spine at the thought.

Within a few days she could be tied to this man for life—taken away from everything she knew and treasured—and her mother would be left alone and defenceless. She couldn't afford to take that risk. She squashed the traitorous thought which had briefly sparked in her brain the previous day, that she would submit to a marriage of convenience if it could be to this man.

That, she told herself, had only happened because of the shock she'd felt when she'd found he was so…different from what she'd expected.

Why, then, had her response to seeing him this morning been even more intense and visceral than yesterday? She was over the shock of seeing him, she told herself. What shocked her now was the behaviour of her own body.

His voice was as reliably deep and measured as she'd remembered it, and the tiny lift at the side of his mouth when she'd referred to their chaperone had sent a dart of forbidden pleasure plunging through her, exactly as she'd known it would.

Now they were walking side-by-side along the gravel path, and she was in charge of showing him some of the garden. Her heart returned to a rhythm more in keeping with someone taking a quick walk, rather than an athlete in the final stages of a marathon, and she returned both her hands to her pockets in case he noticed that they shook a little.

The path curved to the left as it began to slope downward, and Rosabella trod carefully. A slight unevenness in the gravel and the stiff way she held herself threw her a little off-balance and her arm brushed against the Count's. She pulled away sharply, putting more distance between them, but the memory of how it had felt when his hand had rested on her forearm ambushed her again. That delicious rush of shivery sensation must be addictive, she thought and, though she'd spent much of the night dwelling on how his touch had felt and affected her, she knew that the only cure for addiction was total abstinence.

That was all very well in theory. Putting it into practice felt impossible.

CHAPTER EIGHT

THE SUN WAS at its highest, the shadows at their shortest, and Luca and Rosabella were the furthest they'd been from the palace all morning.

Sometime during their walk, the determined pace which the princess had set had slowed to a stroll. Their initial occasional stops to admire the fragrant, waxy blossoms of a frangipani tree, or the red velvet flower of a hibiscus, became increasingly frequent.

Again and again, Luca found himself astonished by Rosabella's detailed knowledge of the flora of Palosia, and her enviable ability to describe it to him with an uncomplicated fluency. He watched her stiff demeanour soften as she lost herself in the place where she obviously felt at ease and in control. As they walked along grassy paths between the borders filled with flowers, she'd reach out to remove a drooping daisy or snap off the pepper-pot seed pod of a poppy, shaking it to sprinkle its seeds onto the earth.

She glanced at him over her shoulder. 'Many

of these plants seed themselves. We have to be vigilant, or the beds become too crowded, but a poppy seed pod is so perfectly designed for its purpose, I can't resist shaking them out.' She'd straightened up, dusting the palms of her hands against the fabric of her dress.

Sometimes she almost seemed to be talking to herself about what they were seeing, but if he asked a question her reply was informed and immediate.

Watching her was almost bewitching. They reached the upper slopes of the citrus orchard, where glossy-leaved orange trees grew in rows, their branches covered in developing fruit.

A few minutes later Luca pointed to a beehive beside the purple haze of a lavender hedge. 'Do you make your own honey?'

'Naturally, we do. The hives are moved according to where the blossom is at its best. Then, when the honeycomb is harvested, we know that it's orange-blossom honey if it's from the orchard, or lavender honey if the hives were near the lavender walk.'

She reached down to pick a flower spike, crushing it between her fingers, and then holding it out to him on the palm of her hand. He inhaled the floral, faintly herbal scent, taking care not to lean too close to her. He wanted to close his hand around hers as she held the crushed bloom, but he kept his hands in his pockets.

'Mmm. It's exquisite. The honey must be exceptionally good.'

'Honey from Palosia is rare and prized.' She dropped the petals to the ground. 'If you like, I'll ask the head gardener to give you some to take back to Tuscany.'

'I'd like that very much. Thank you.'

The moment felt intimate and precious, as if she'd finally accepted that he was a real person who might like a simple thing like honey, not a stranger who'd come to finalise the business of marrying her. It seemed as if they'd moved beyond formality, and the unspoken thing that hung between them.

Their eyes met and for the first time she didn't look away. The air was warm, and thick with the sound of assiduous bees and the call of birds, but Luca felt that the beat of his heart and the rush of his blood must be loud enough for her to hear. He had the strangest feeling that if he reached out and cupped her cheek in his palm she might not recoil.

Fascinated, he watched her guarded expression change to one of confusion and then, he was sure, to one of curiosity. He hardly dared breathe.

A loud cough broke the spell. Luca almost heard the snap as the tension in the air broke, and with a jolt he remembered the presence of the chaperone. He exhaled a long breath. For a moment in which time had appeared to stretch, the world had shrunk to just the two of them and the emotion that hummed between them. He'd completely forgotten that their every move was being observed.

He'd allowed the intoxicating scents and sounds of the garden to overwhelm his senses and cloud his famously sharp mind. The fact that he was the focus of attention of this beautiful princess had not helped him to maintain his equilibrium. He was a world away from his usual comfort zone, he rationalised; immersed in an exotic environment, in the unlikely position of getting to know the woman who was meant to become his wife.

It felt crazy. He had to get his thoughts and feelings back into some sort of balance before he did something he'd regret that would make the task at hand much, much more difficult. Apart from the practicalities of having to extract himself from the absurd marriage deal, he wanted with all his heart not to do anything that would allow Rosabella to believe he might have feelings for her.

Naturally, he did not. He'd met her barely twenty-four hours ago, unless he counted their brief encounter twenty *years* ago, and that would be ridiculous. This impulse to touch her, to feel the softness of her skin under his hands, to *kiss* her even, was all the result of the romantic location, the heady scent of the blossom and the presence of a beautiful princess. What man would *not* want to kiss her?

He clenched his fists in his pockets. Frustration tugged at him, but he knew he could do nothing to release it here. Later, when it was cooler, he'd go for a run in the hills, or swim fifty laps of the pool he'd glimpsed from his windows. Better still, he'd arrange a meeting with King Fiero and get this over with before it became more complicated than it already was.

The chaperone coughed again, and Luca looked over at her. She tapped the watch on her wrist.

He returned his full attention to the princess. Her bottom lip was caught between her teeth. She looked cool and calm, but he could see the rapid beat of the little pulse at her throat.

'I think,' he said quietly, 'We're being given our instructions. It must be midday.' He glanced up at the sun, almost directly overhead. 'And we still have to walk back up to the palace. I'm afraid I've kept you out in the heat for too long.'

Rosabella shook her head. 'No, I'm perfectly used to it, although it's our custom to stay out of the sun during the hottest part of the day. Yesterday, I…'

'Yesterday you didn't have your hat.'

'Luckily, I remembered it today.'

She turned towards him, and at last he was rewarded with the wide smile she'd handed him the previous morning. He thought it hinted that they were complicit in something.

The walk back up to the palace was steep, and once they'd left the citrus orchard behind there was little shade. Their chaperone puffed up the slopes ahead of them, obviously satisfied that her duties were complete. Only once did she look back to check on them.

Despite the heat, Rosabella felt filled with a strange exhilaration. The morning had flown by, and she found herself wishing that it wasn't over yet. Count Luca had expressed interest in every aspect of the things she'd shown him and had asked searching, intelligent questions.

It was enjoyable to hold a conversation with an adult who was not one of her parents or a member of the court. The ever-present dull ache of missing her sister flared. This man who walked beside her, attentive to her words as well as her physical comfort, sharpened her awareness of everything. He seemed to enjoy her company and to find the things she said interesting. How he made her feel was new and exciting. She must make the most of his company, while she could.

Once he'd gone, and she'd told her father she would never marry for convenience, to cement an alliance or to satisfy the ego or ambition of a man, she could expect a life of doing…probably very little. She had not been allowed to pursue her dream of becoming a garden designer, or anything else. Further education, her father had thundered, was wasted on women. All they needed to do was be wives and mothers, preferably to sons, but some of them couldn't even get that right.

How thrilling it must be for her sister finally to be able to fulfil her ambition to forge a career in interior design. Rosabella had become more and more responsible for her fragile mother's care. Her role in the charities her mother had founded, to help women and children access education and develop skills that would allow them to support themselves, would steadily increase.

Not that she minded. She loved her twice-weekly visits to the workshop they had established, where they'd revived the centuries-old craft of making hats from the left-over straw from the wheat harvest. The women wove intricate hats that they were beginning export to far corners of the world. A small school had been set up as part of the enterprise where the workers' children were taught by volunteer retired teachers.

What had begun as an experiment was now a thriving business, and Rosa found the days she spent there deeply fulfilling. Working with the women, taking orders from foreign buyers and sourcing materials and new designs made her feel alive and useful—as if she was doing something useful, rather than just marking time until her twenty-fifth birthday, when her life was due to change dramatically.

Would her father allow her to expand her role at the workshop when she refused to marry a man who would never love her back? Given his views on education and employment for women, it was unlikely, but it was something for which she was prepared to fight. She'd been denied the opportunity to follow the career of her choice, in garden design, but she could help other women realise their potential and achieve their ambitions.

Perhaps the rewards she'd reap from helping others would, over time, help her to accept a life without love.

She'd be at the hat workshop in two days' time, and the thought brought a little warmth to the coldness which had settled around her heart as they reached the top of the steps, near the archway. Was this the moment when she really would bid farewell to Count Luca for the last time? Although Luisa had said he planned to stay, there was nothing to stop him from changing his plans. He might have found the morning…okay, her company…boring. His interest in the gardens had most likely been fabricated, just to give him something to talk about with a freckle-faced, unsophisticated woman.

The confidence she'd felt walking and talking with him began to crumble and she stood, tongue-tied and awkward, waiting for him to make an excuse to leave.

The chaperone disappeared through a side door to the palace. Did her father honestly believe that she had been necessary? After all, he'd spent enough time telling her that no man would ever fall in love with her, and demonstrating, by his habit of ignoring her at all other times, that she was unlovable. Why did he think that the Count might be the exception to prove that rule?

Then she remembered how her half-sister's disappearance had unfolded. King Fiero had been left humiliated and furious by Sofia's defiant desertion. He was not going to let that happen again.

Rosabella tried not to think too often about her beloved half-sister because the ache of loss was almost too much to bear. Sofia had been her friend, companion and protector, often standing between Rosabella and their father when he'd raged that she was a useless girl who should have been a boy. She'd been afraid that Rosa's mother would abandon her, as her own had done.

The times they had been apart had been hard, but she'd always come back. Not this time, though. She had married the love of her life and gone from Palosia for good. Rosa was happy for her—she truly was—but that didn't stop her from missing her, every day.

Sofia had deserted Prince Eduardo, the man the King had chosen for her, at the altar. Marriage to him would have cemented an important alliance between Palosia and the prince's own ancient dynasty of Sarcos, on a neighbouring island. Then she had found Marco again. Her sister's bravery had given Rosa the courage to make her own decision. She wasn't yet sure from where she'd find the great courage she'd need to carry it out. She would not marry the man her father had chosen for her either, but sadly, in her case, she had no-one like Marco to find.

With anyone else the silence which stretched between her and the Count would have felt awkward, but it seemed he was comfortable enough not to feel he had to fill it. She looked across the valley, where heat shimmered on the clay-tiled rooftops of the village below. The mist had cleared from the mountain tops, leaving their rocky peaks etched against the clear blue sky. The distant sea shimmered, the sunlight dancing off the glittering waves.

A prickle of awareness brought her attention back to the Count, and she knew he was looking at her. Feeling his eyes on her made her chest feel unnaturally tight and she took a big breath, trying to ease it. She swallowed hard, as if she might be able to stop the sensations that rose through her, threatening to morph into words which she'd be embarrassed by and regret later.

'Thank you for this morning, Princess Rosabella. I've enjoyed it much more than… I can express. May I ask you something?'

She went still, dreading what might be coming. Was he about to ruin the hours they'd spent together by mentioning the marriage? It felt to her as if they'd both avoided the subject by silent mutual agreement, but perhaps she'd completely misread the situation. She had no experience of how these matters worked. How could she respond to him with honesty when she had no intention of going through with their wedding?

But he surprised her.

'Where did you learn about horticulture? Your knowledge seems extensive, at least to a layman like me. Have you been to university? Studied botany?'

Relief washed over her and she smiled, even though her lack of formal education was something she regretted and resented. This question was an easy one to answer.

'From my mother. She rescued these gardens from years of neglect and she has passed on her knowledge to me.'

'Ah.' He nodded. 'I remember you telling me, all those years ago, that your mother was a gardener. What you did not tell me was that she was also the Queen.' A half-smile teased his mouth. 'I simply assumed that she was one of the team of gardeners which must be needed to keep this estate in order.'

'Twenty years ago, if that was when we met as children, she would only have wrestled a small part of them back from nature. The maze had been here for centuries, and she restored that first.'

'Does she still manage the gardens? Yesterday, she seemed...frail.'

Rosabella looked down at her feet. Her sandals were dusty and a stalk of grass was lodged under one of the straps. They weren't suitable for the sort of walk they'd done, but Luisa had prevailed in the shoe battle that morning and insisted she wear them, rather than her canvas plimsols.

'No.' She bent to tug the stalk free and rolled it between her fingers. 'She walks on the level paths sometimes, and she sits in the shade of the old linden tree.'

He followed her gaze and saw the tree she indicated. Its twisted trunk was gnarled with age and there was a wooden bench beneath it in the deep shade cast by its canopy.

'She no longer plays an active part but her knowledge is boundless.'

'Did she study the subject? I'm afraid I'm rather ignorant of the achievements of your family.'

Rosabella laughed. 'She's entirely self-taught. I think my grandfather's attitude towards education for women was even more antiquated than my own father's. Her life was completely sheltered until she married him, and not a lot changed.' She shrugged. 'I think she found solace…'

She stopped, wishing she could take the words back. She'd said too much. The way her father treated her mother was shameful and private, not something to be discussed with a stranger. If it wasn't for the fact that the citizens of Palosia sympathised with her and loved her for the charitable work she did among them, King Fiero might well have divorced her and taken another wife in his bid to have a son.

'Solace?'

Any hope she'd had that he might have missed what she'd said evaporated on the warm air. She took a quick step back, putting what she hoped was a safer distance between them. She'd allowed him to get too close, not just in body but in mind. He'd made her feel too comfortable, and she'd dropped her guard. If the chaperone hadn't reminded them of her presence in the orchard…

She didn't know what might have happened, because she had nothing on which to base her imagination, but she'd *wanted* something to happen.

Was it wrong of her to long to discover how it felt to be wanted, or cherished, even if it was only once in her life?

She felt a shiver of apprehension. He'd have soon discovered that she had no experience or expertise in the art of flirting. That, she thought bitterly, would have been a quick route to persuading him that he really did not want to marry her.

A breeze had picked up and it lifted the brim of her hat. She put a hand on the crown to keep it in place.

'I need to go. Thank you for your company this morning...' She found she didn't know how to finish. Should she say goodbye, as if she did not expect to see him again? Flustered, she spun round and walked away.

He didn't call after her, yet he'd mentioned tomorrow...

Luca watched her retreating. Her steps were hurried, her back stiff and straight. So much effort seemed to be expended in keeping up the appearance of strength and determination, that it had the effect of making her look achingly vulnerable.

On their tour of the garden, he'd been fascinated to see how she'd unwound, bit by bit, until he'd found it easy to converse with her and ask questions about the plants, trees and flowers. The garden was obviously her happy place. Her mother had found *solace* in her restoration project. Had she passed on that solace to her daughter? And why did either of them need it?

Palosia should have felt like an island paradise, yet the King was bad-tempered, the Queen frail and anxious and Rosabella did her best to hide her vulnerability behind a shield of stiff control. What he'd believed would be a quick, if rather brutal, transaction between himself and the King could turn into something much more complicated if he allowed his concern for the princess to get in the way.

He did not owe them anything, he told himself, although he admitted that money might have to change hands if he was to extricate himself from the proposed marriage. He was okay with that, and the quicker he put his plans in motion the better.

But a weight of responsibility pressed down on him in the form of the future welfare of Princess Rosabella. If he'd chosen a different path in life, it might not have affected him in this way, but he was a lawyer who defended members of society who were defenceless against the lot life had dealt them. For him, it was an impossibility to stand by and watch another human being suffer if he could do something to alleviate that suffering.

While this family of ancient noble lineage appeared to have it all—wealth, a home of such opulence that most people could never dream of, security and an island kingdom of stunning beauty and abundance—unhappiness pervaded the very atmosphere of the place. It had been obvious how Rosabella's spirits had lifted, her whole demeanour changed, when she'd talked to him about the garden. Amongst the flowers and trees, she was in her true element, filled with enthusiasm for and a love of nature.

Standing in the citrus orchard, he'd felt a surge of feeling for her, and the urge to cup her cheek in his palm, to feel the petal-softness of her skin, had been almost overwhelming. The look in her eyes had told him she had wanted something too. But as they'd climbed back towards the palace, and a parting of their ways, he'd watched her revert to her cool, guarded self.

It was a cardinal rule never, ever to become personally involved with a client. Crossing that line clouded judgement, destroyed impartiality and closed the gap that was essential to maintain clear-sightedness. It was something of which he had never been guilty. He ran a tight ship, and it ensured his continued reputation as one of the best.

He watched Princess Rosabella vanish through

the French windows across the courtyard and huffed out a sigh of frustration. What was going on with him? Why was he finding this difficult? Everything should have been done and dusted by now and he should have been back in his castle—which he would hardly call home—at his penthouse in Rome, or even on his way back to New York.

Why was it that not one of those prospects filled him with even a hint of pleasure? Could he make allowances for this feeling of wanting to tear up the rule book because the princess was not a client, and therefore the rules did not apply to her? She was meant to become his *wife*, damn it.

His brain stalled at that thought. The idea that he'd even permitted it to form felt dangerous, putting all he held true and certain in jeopardy. She could never be his wife. Never. His father had duped him for twenty years and had gone to his grave believing he'd defeated him. Luca would go to his own knowing he'd triumphed over the control and bullying that had robbed him of his mother. The rage he harboured for his father was corrosive, but he welcomed the bitter taste it brought to his mouth. It served to focus his mind.

He couldn't—*wouldn't*—allow concern for this enigmatic princess to undermine his stated purpose.

Later, Luca asked the valet who'd been assigned to see to his needs to have his hire car brought to him. He urgently needed to put some distance between Rosabella and himself, and strenuous physical activity was the quickest way he knew to suppress inconvenient desire.

Since he'd originally planned to stay on Palosia for less than twenty-four hours, he hadn't packed for a holiday. He decided to drive down to the village, buy swimming things and find a beach where he could swim until he'd worn himself out. That way he just might be able to clear his mind of the image of deep-brown eyes, faint freckles on a straight nose and hair he longed to loosen from its restraining braid and run his fingers through before cupping her face in his hands...

He slammed the car door and pressed the ignition button, then he lowered the soft top. Getting the wind in his face might help. The solid roar of the engine was satisfying as he released the brake and pressed the accelerator. This car was something solid and predictable which behaved as he expected it to. He could control its power and speed and the direction it would take.

The realisation that his own mind and body were not so reliably biddable shocked him.

CHAPTER NINE

When Luisa carried Rosabella's breakfast tray onto the balcony the following morning, she brought no message from Luca.

From behind the dark protection of her sunglasses, Rosabella studied her face, searching for clues but coming up with nothing. Luisa's face was impassive, and Rosabella refused to bow to her own need and ask for news of him.

Luisa ran her eye over Rosabella's clothes and clicked her tongue in what could have been frustration.

Rosabella rose to the bait. 'What is it, Luisa? If I've offended you, I apologise, but please tell me what I've done so that I can make sure I don't do it again.'

Luisa smiled. 'No, of course you haven't offended me, and if you had I'd certainly explain how. It's just…' She sighed. 'You have so many pretty clothes.'

'Since I'm planning another day in the garden, I don't need anything pretty.'

'You were in the garden yesterday, and you wore that lovely dress.'

'That was because I had to play hostess to my father's guest.' She bent a leg up and hugged her knee. 'Today, I'll be working.'

'But the Count...'

'Since he has not asked to see me today, I presume he's left. And without saying goodbye.'

She wished she hadn't said that. It might sound as if she cared, and she didn't.

On her way back through the doorway, Luisa turned. 'I don't know what he plans to do today, but he hasn't left—not yet. There might still be time.'

Rosabella snapped her head round to look at her, all kinds of scenarios rushing through her head. 'Time for what, exactly?'

'Oh, time for him to say goodbye. After all, his manners are beyond reproach.'

The work of tying in the thorny stems of a climbing rose that scrambled over a wrought-iron frame was hot, hard and scratchy, but the scent of the pale-pink blooms intensified as the day grew warmer and more than compensated for her aching shoulders.

Rosabella ducked under the dense growth into welcome shade, where water trickled into a stone basin. She dropped her hat onto the paving stones, pulled off her gardening gloves and wiped the beads of perspiration from her forehead. Then she scooped up water in her cupped hands and splashed it over her face. She sighed as the cool drops trickled down her neck. She tucked a strand of hair behind her ear, then she sat down to rest on the cushioned swing seat to admire the view over the flower garden.

'Is this a good time? It looks as if you're taking a break.'

Every muscle in Rosabella's body stilled, apart from her irritating heart, which began to hammer against her ribs. It felt as if her chest might not have enough space for it. Her lungs squeezed and her breathing quickened. The fingers that she'd pushed into her hair at her temples were stiff. His voice took her thoughts to the dark, amber honey that they harvested from the hives near the meadow, where the buckwheat grew wild.

She was dirty and sweaty, and a scratch on her arm was caked with dried blood. Luisa's words beat in her brain: *You have so many pretty clothes*. She was most comfortable in what she wore now, but her skirt and top showed her exactly as she was. They didn't provide a disguise, like a pretty dress did. She lowered her hands and slid her fingers into her pockets before turning.

Luca stood at the entrance to the arbour. She blinked, because the light beyond him was dazzling and all she could see was his silhouette against the summer sky. But the shape of those wide shoulders was already imprinted on her mind.

'I... Yes.' She tried to swallow the constriction in her throat, to find a voice that sounded more like hers. 'That is, yes, I'm taking a break.' She lifted her shoulders. 'But a good time for what?'

Her mind, which had frozen along with most of the rest of her, leapt back into action. What did he want? Did he want to talk about the marriage? Or had he come to tell her he was leaving, as good manners dictated that he should?

He stepped out of the light into the shade and Rosabella remembered that this was one of the places she was not going to show him. She'd decided to tidy up this arbour today because it was in a remote corner of the garden where she'd felt sure she'd be undisturbed. After the stress of the last two days, she craved time to herself to reset and put her thoughts and feelings back where they belonged, under control.

He looked a lot more relaxed than she felt. The black jeans he wore were comfortably worn-in; his grey tee-shirt clung to his shoulders and the flat planes of his stomach and abdomen, not hiding anything of his physique.

'Oh,' he said, his tone light. 'Just to continue our conversation from yesterday, but without...'

He glanced over his shoulder towards the entrance.

Rosabella's eyes followed his. 'You mean... there's no-one *else* here?'

'Uh-huh.' He shrugged. 'No chaperone.' His lips lifted at the corners and her stomach dropped, doing a curious loop-the-loop on the way. It settled low down, leaving a hollow where she felt it should have been. She was convinced the beat of her heart could be heard. It could definitely be seen, if he looked.

'How did you find me?' Did he suspect she'd been hiding from him? The physical exertions of the morning had given her mind time and space to consider, and she'd convinced herself that she really didn't care if the Count had left. It would mean she could now tell her father her decision. She was tired of putting off the confrontation and afraid that, with each day which passed, a little of her determination would ebb away.

He made her feel things she'd never felt before, but then she'd never had the opportunity. Perhaps that sense of the world receding and her focus narrowing to one specific point, or feeling she'd willingly do anything he asked of her when he looked into her eyes was perfectly normal when a man touched her arm. To *want* to do anything for him.

The often-present longing for her sister squeezed

her heart a little more tightly. They'd always talked to each other, and she wished she could talk to her about this. Sofia knew about love, courage and following one's own path. She'd be able to reassure her and tell her that these feelings meant nothing at all.

'I asked one of the gardeners. He said he'd seen you heading this way.' His eyes dropped and she knew he'd seen her chest rise and heard her sigh of annoyance. 'Did you not want to be found? I can leave.'

'No, please don't.' She shook her head and a lock of her hair fell across her forehead. 'It's just that I feel as if someone is always tracking my movements. I'm probably over-sensitive.'

Her cheeks were flushed and there was a damp patch on the front of her shirt, making it stick to her skin. He sat down on the stone wall at the front of the arbor to distract himself. She seemed oblivious to the effect she was having on him. He felt as warm as she looked, only it wasn't from the sun or hard work. He stretched out his legs and crossed them at the ankles, resting his hands behind him on the stone parapet in a show of seeming relaxation.

'I wanted to ask you,' he said, raising his eyes to her face, 'About your hat.'

Rosabella glanced down at her straw hat. It

was the battered one she only wore for gardening, unlike the elegant, broad-brimmed and intricately woven one she'd worn the previous day.

'Which hat?' Her brows drew together. 'That one, or the one I wore yesterday?'

'Both.' He leaned forward and propped his folded arms on his thighs. 'Yesterday afternoon I decided to explore a little. I drove down to the village in the valley. I went swimming in the sea, I...'

'Swimming?'

'Do you like swimming?'

She nodded. A spark, possibly of longing, lit her eyes. 'I love swimming. But I haven't swum in the sea for a long time. When I was a child, I used to challenge myself to dive off the rocks into the sea. I thought that if I climbed higher and dived deeper, my father...' She stopped and gave a quick shake of her head.

'You thought what—that he'd be afraid for you?'

She laughed, and there was bitterness in the sound. 'That he might *notice* me.'

He nodded, understanding far more from her few words than she probably realised. The anger that had gripped him last night—so fiercely that he'd had difficulty stopping himself from barging into the King's study and tearing up the despicable marriage agreement under his nose—roared back.

Last night, he'd returned to the palace, tired from a strenuous swim in the surf and a couple of miles of running on the beach, followed by a meal at a beachside café. He'd put his thoughts in order and settled his mind. He'd decided he would talk to King Fiero in the morning. Having made his case clear to the monarch, he would ask permission to dine with Princess Rosabella and explain to her, in as gentle a way as possible, why they could never be married. And then he would leave.

He'd showered and then done what he should have done as soon as this situation had come to light. He'd settled down to read the marriage document from beginning to end with as much detachment as he could muster. It was imperative that he had all the facts at his fingertips when he approached King Fiero.

At first it appeared to be a straightforward document, if a contract for a marriage of convenience could ever be called that. He and the princess were to be married when she turned twenty-five. He frowned at the nearness of the date. Just how much notice of the event had his father been planning to give him? And what would have happened if he hadn't returned to Tuscany and found the document when his father had died? The fact that they were estranged was an open secret and nobody would have been surprised if he hadn't attended the funeral. Would

King Fiero have sent a couple of his acolytes to New York or Rome to find him and bring him to Palosia to fulfil his, or rather his *father*'s, side of the bargain? He'd smiled grimly at the idea.

But then he'd got onto the small print, and he'd stopped smiling.

It seemed Rosabella would leave Palosia as soon as they were married, to live with him in Tuscany. The expectation of a male heir was clear. When the anticipated boy was two, he'd be taken from her, along with any rights his parents had, and returned to the island to be raised by the King as his heir.

The prince, if one was born, would have no memory of his mother. Luca knew that with the authority of one who'd lost his own mother at that same age. The difference was that he'd been cared for by his kind and thoughtful grandparents, in a home filled with love and mutual respect. In his mind, their marriage and relationship was a shining example to him of what love and commitment looked like.

If he ever married, it would be for love and for ever, not to appease a king who clearly saw his daughter simply as a nuisance to be removed from his life. But also someone to provide an heir, or to fulfil the egotistical longing of his father to ally his name with that of an ancient kingdom.

What sort of lonely, frightening life would a little boy taken over by King Fiero have? He had only to look at the frail, shadow of a woman that was the Queen to understand the effects of the man's unreasonable expectations and bullying tactics.

Even if he *wanted* to marry Princess Rosabella, the terms of this agreement would make that impossible. He could never agree to it. He did not want to marry her, but he was beginning to realise that he cared about her.

Now he stood up abruptly, trying to keep his fury at bay. If he gave vent to it and said what was on his mind, he would frighten her. He dragged a hand over his face and felt the scrape of stubble on his jaw. He'd slept badly, with this appalling information churning in his mind, and then had fallen into a fitful sleep as dawn had begun to lighten the sky. He hadn't bothered to shave when he'd finally risen, and had drunk two cups of strong black coffee.

It was late morning when he'd stepped out into the sun to find Princess Rosabella. He'd felt an irrational need to reassure himself that she was alright—though what harm could possibly have come to her in less than twenty-four hours? And yet, what if her father had been dissatisfied with the report back from their disgruntled chaperone? What if Rosabella had been deemed to have been too forward with him, or perhaps not forward enough? Not all damage had to have a physical face, he thought grimly.

If the princess would agree, he needed to get her away from the claustrophobic and watchful atmosphere of the palace. He'd only be able to talk freely to her where she could forget about the possibilities of staff eavesdropping on their conversation.

He spent too long wrapped in his thoughts and now she was watching him, two faint lines between her eyebrows, as if she was trying to predict what he might do or say next.

'You mentioned my hat?' Her voice was soft, as though she felt she had to tread gently or risk him cracking in some way.

He nodded, dragging himself back to the present, and the realisation that whatever he did, he'd be destroying her happiness. The weight of that knowledge would be impossible to carry and ever feel free again.

'I went into a boutique to buy a towel and swimming trunks. They had straw hats like yours on sale, and I noticed that they were made on Palosia. They're very beautiful. Can you tell me about them?'

Rosabella bent, retrieved her gardening hat from the stone paving and handed it to him. It was woven from coarse straw, with a rounded crown and up-turned brim. An iridescent blue feather was stuck under the green ribbon that was tied around it.

'Hats have been woven on Palosia for hundreds of years, but the art had been all but lost by the turn of the century. It's thanks to my mother that it's been revived.'

'Your *mother*?'

Her expression had become guarded. 'Why would you want to know about hats?'

He conceded to himself that her question was a fair one. Why would he want to know? But it wasn't really the hats; it was Rosabella he wanted to know about.

'Because you wear them, and I'm interested in you.'

Her watchful expression vanished but the incredulity which replaced it tugged at his heart.

'I thought you were here to finalise things… with my father. Not to be interested in me.'

He nodded and tried to keep his tone neutral. 'I accept that my intention was to discuss matters with your father. But now I want to discuss things with you. Only, not here.' He looked around, spreading his hands. 'I'd like to take you out—have a proper conversation. Obviously, I'd have to ask permission from your father, but I can't see that he'd refuse.'

'No, he wouldn't refuse. But he might make

sure he had eyes and ears at the next table.' She reached out and took her hat back from him, turning it in her hands. 'But,' she said, 'If you really want to know about the hats…'

Her voice wavered, and he wanted to remove the hat, take her hands in his and make her lift her gaze from where it was fixed on a spot on the stone slabs beneath their feet, and meet his. 'I have another idea.'

CHAPTER TEN

Rosabella busied herself with the display of hats in the reception area of the Palosia hat workshop. A volunteer receptionist manned the desk, next to the double doors which led to the small manufacturing unit. She'd positioned herself between the desk and the entrance so that she could greet Luca when he arrived.

If he arrived.

She glanced at her watch for the tenth time. It was five minutes past the time they'd arranged and she decided to give him another five before concluding that he definitely wasn't coming.

Today was one of the two she spent at the charity each week, and it was her favourite time. One of the palace drivers had dropped her off at eight o'clock that morning and, as usual, the time had flown.

Until now.

She'd done her usual round of the busy factory floor, where some women were weaving straw into braids and others were turning those braids into rudimentary hat shapes, using wooden blocks of varying sizes. In a separate room, the final designs were being created. Some were bespoke orders, while others were destined for boutiques, such as the one the Count had visited, or to fulfil orders from abroad.

Finally, she put her head round the door of the crèche and then the school room, where the children of employees were cared for and taught.

The glass entrance door swung open again but she did not look up. She was bound to be disappointed.

Luca saw her immediately. She stood before a display of elegant hats woven of fine straw in different colours. They were the sort of hats which could have been seen at any famous race meeting or royal garden party, and a far cry from the battered model which Rosabella had worn in the garden.

She was dressed in a soft linen skirt and a cream blouse with a rounded collar. Her hair was pulled into a messy bun, secured with clips that sported tiny butterflies. His eyes followed the movements of her elegant hands as she adjusted the position of a particularly spectacular, bright-red hat.

'Good morning.'

She looked up and their eyes clashed, and he

was rewarded with another of those wide, dimpled smiles he craved.

'You came.' She stood up, straightening her skirt and putting a hand to her hair.

'Did you doubt it?'

'No...yes. To be honest, I did think you might change your mind.'

'Why would I do that? I wanted to see you. And to learn about the hats.'

She took him on a tour of the premises, answering his questions. The industrious atmosphere impressed him, and the childcare facilities impressed him more, but what intrigued him the most was the difference in Rosabella. Rather like the changed person she became in the garden, she was engaged in what she was doing, ready to talk to him with passion and without reserve about what she showed him. She knew all the workers and their children by name and demonstrated care and respect for them. Her interest in them was obviously reciprocated. Many of the women asked after the Queen with concern.

When they'd concluded the tour, he bought them coffee from the work canteen and carried the tray out into a small garden. Tables and chairs were grouped under shady trees and tubs of crimson geraniums marked the edges of the paths.

'My mother established this outdoor space.' Rosabella led the way to a table, stopping to pick a yellowing leaf from a plant. 'There's a children's play area too.' She nodded towards a climbing frame and swings. 'For Palosia, at the time it was innovative, but many other businesses have followed her lead.'

They sat opposite each other and Luca placed a mug of coffee in front of her. 'Thank you. My mother is much loved and respected.'

'Yes, I can see that. Do you know what motivated her?'

Rosabella's face clouded and she dropped her gaze, tucking a strand of hair behind an ear.

'I suppose she…needed a distraction. She started by beginning to restore the palace gardens, and then she had this idea.'

'A distraction from what?' He tried to hold her gaze, but she looked away. He watched her chest rise on a deep breath and he thought she was going to shake her head and rebuff his question. She wrapped both her hands round the coffee mug, her knuckles whitening, raised it and took a sip before replacing it carefully on the table.

'From the fact that my birth had robbed her of the chance to have any more children. And I wasn't a boy.' When she looked up at him again, her expression was stricken. She shook her head. 'I'm sorry. I shouldn't have said that. It's not something you need to know.'

There was a deep sadness in her that he wanted

to understand, and perhaps alleviate. Understanding people who had been traumatised by events over which they'd had no control was something he did very well. He should be able to do it for Rosabella. The connection he was beginning to feel to her should make it easier, but instead he found himself hesitating, searching for the right words, aware that getting this right was terribly important—although the reason he felt that way hovered at the edge of his mind, just out of reach.

'Rosabella... May I call you that?'

She nodded, the line of her jaw tense, her hands still gripping the mug. 'Most people call me Rosa.'

'Rosa, then. And you must call me Luca.'

She darted a look at him. 'I...don't know if I can.'

'Try. You'll see it isn't so difficult.' Very gently, he lifted her fingers away from the mug. 'I'm afraid you're going to crush that mug.' He placed her hands on the table. 'Say it, just once. Nobody else is listening.'

She took a couple of breaths. 'Luca?' she whispered, and then half-smiled. 'Luca.'

'See?' He lifted his own mug and swallowed a mouthful of coffee. 'Not so difficult. Now, tell me why you've taken your mother's guilt and regret onto your own shoulders. Because I think that is what you've done.'

Luca thought he knew the answer, but he knew that persuading victims to articulate their feelings themselves could help to rationalise their thoughts.

Rosabella's eyes were fixed on her hands, and he had the strong feeling that she wished he'd kept holding them. He'd wanted to. He'd wanted to turn her hands over in his and stroke his thumbs across her palms and the pale insides of her wrists, but he knew how alien a man's touch was to her. Most of all, he wanted her to feel in control.

'Because it was my fault.'

He had to lean in to hear her.

'Why else?'

'How we're born and whether we're girls or boys are two things over which we have zero control. Someone has imposed that guilt on you all your life.' He leaned back in his chair, mentally reaching for the self-control that would enable him to keep anger from his voice. 'I'm guessing it was your father,' he ground out, his jaw rigid.

What looked like a self-deprecating smile curved her lips and she nodded. 'Of course, logically I know I wasn't to blame, but emotionally... Until quite recently 'what if' was something I asked myself frequently.'

'What did you wish could be different?'

'I wished—still wish—that my father did not resent us...my sister and me, or our mothers.'

Surprise made Luca's eyes snap back to hers. 'You have a *sister*?'

'A half-sister—Sofia. Her mother was our father's first wife. She was very beautiful, but not of royal blood, and she ran away after Sofia was born, back to her true love.' She nipped at her bottom lip. 'My father divorced and banished her and married my mother very quickly afterwards, needing a son to secure the succession, since the law of Palosia states that only a male can rule. But he got me, and after that my mother couldn't have any more children. So, you see...well, you see how it could be blamed on me.'

Luca did see, very clearly, and he wanted to punch something, or someone. His hands curled, his fingernails biting into his palms. The reason for Rosabella being offered in a marriage of convenience from an early age suddenly made sense, given the restricted and old-fashioned world of Palosia. And the draconian clause enabling her father to take away a baby son from her, to be raised by him, was the brutal attempt of a man who needed to keep control at all costs trying to order things to enable him to exercise it.

'Where is your sister now?' He hardly dared ask the question.

'She refused to marry the prince our father

had chosen for her when she discovered he loved someone else. The union would have cemented an important alliance, but she left her fiancé at the altar, fled to Naples and found the man she'd loved since she was twenty—when she ran away to search for her mother. In the end, she married…for love.'

Her voice cracked and Luca wanted to put his arms around her, stroke her hair and hold her hands—anything to sooth that ragged break in her voice that said almost more than her words could.

After that disaster, the King would have felt humiliated and out of control of his own family and his kingdom. No wonder, then, that Rosa was subjected to such close scrutiny and her movements so restricted. The King was doing everything humanly possible to prevent a repeat performance and to ensure that, if Rosa gave birth to a son, he would have control over him.

'Are you in touch with Sofia? Where is she?'

'Yes, but she and Marco, her husband, are both involved in their businesses. Sofia is an interior designer now, and he's the CEO of Krafty. He set it up as an online marketplace for small businesses and entrepreneurs, but it grew very quickly. Marco is hugely successful.'

'Sofia is married to Marco Stewart?' Luca blew out a breath. 'That's amazing. In my legal work I frequently cite Krafty as a model for relationships between management and employees. They have an excellent record in that regard, and for their equal opportunities ethos. It's massively successful on a global scale. Marco Stewart is a very wealthy man.'

'When Sofia first met him, he was a poor artist training to be a sculptor. The thing is, Sofia didn't believe in love. Her mother abandoned her when she was one, so she always felt unloved and unlovable. Our father didn't help, banishing her mother and wiping Sofia from the line of succession, even if she had a son. But she had the courage to stand up to him and for her rights. Love found her and she embraced it, in spite of everything.'

Luca felt an unfamiliar sensation in his chest, as if his heart were being squeezed tight and his lungs crushed. He sucked in a deep, deliberate breath, trying to ease the feeling. Was this what Rosa hoped for? That love would find her, even though she was being forced into a marriage of convenience designed to ensure the succession and bolster the ego of his now dead father? He remembered the flash of what he'd interpreted as hope in her eyes, and he needed to take another breath.

She had all the qualities anyone could wish for: beauty, kindness, generosity and thoughtfulness.

And, from his tour of the factory, he'd learned that she cared very much for the people of Palosia. He did not doubt that she had a deep capacity for love. Not only would she make a wonderful partner, but she'd also be a great ruler, if her narrow-minded and autocratic father could only see beyond the boundaries of the antiquated and self-centred conventions that bound him.

Rosa deserved all the love in the world, but he could not give it to her. By binding Luca to her in a betrothal of convenience to boost his own ego and wealth, his father had made sure of that. Anger churned in his stomach. Rosa needed someone to love her unconditionally, not a husband who had been forced on her for the sake of convenience. The battle he'd fought against his father's control had been hard won, and he wasn't about to concede defeat by consenting to the marriage agreement.

Luca's lips were pressed together in a straight line, his jaw taut, and anger seemed to fight a battle with compassion in his dark eyes. But Rosa's attention was dragged away from his face to the drumming of his fingers on the table. His breathing was steady but deep, as if by concentrating on every breath he was controlling whatever it was that had angered him.

She wished he'd continued to hold her hands.

Luca's hands on hers had been gentle yet sure. The touch of his fingers had sent *that* sensation buzzing up her arms and down into the pit of her stomach, where it had settled into a feeling of yearning and anticipation of what might have come next, if circumstances had been different.

Above all, his light caress had rekindled that sensation of being safe. Perhaps that was why she longed for it to continue. The urge to lace her fingers through his, to anchor herself to him, to prolong that sense of security, was powerful.

The coffee was cold but she lifted the mug and took another sip, just to give her hands something to do in case they reached over to cover his drumming fingers. She glanced across at him and he closed his eyes for a second, then leaned back in his chair and raked his fingers through his hair, before folding his arms across his chest.

His fingers tapped against his biceps. He'd rolled up his shirtsleeves to the elbows, revealing tanned, muscled forearms and a slim watch on his wrist. Dazedly, Rosabella wondered about the time and, as if reading her mind, Luca glanced at his watch.

'It's just after midday. How soon can you get away?'

'Get away?' She wasn't sure she'd heard him correctly. 'I don't "get away". The palace driver will collect me. If there's any shopping I need to

do, he'll take me to the appropriate stores and wait for me, then he'll take me back to the palace.'

'Seriously?'

She nodded. 'When Sofia ran away the first time, I was sixteen and still very much restricted to the palace and the gardens. But when she fled from her wedding my father became even more paranoid. He's convinced I'll try to run away too, to join Sofia. It's a little better since Sofia married, but he keeps track of what I'm doing. That's why the garden, and the two days a week I spend here, are so precious to me.'

She looked at him, hoping he might understand. 'He knows where I am, so I'm left alone and I can feel a little...free.'

Luca leaned forward and rested his forearms on the table, holding her gaze with his.

'With your permission, I'll cancel the driver and take you back to the palace when you're ready. When *we're* ready.'

'But my father...'

'I'll send a message to your father with the driver. He may not like it, but he'll accept it. He agreed we should take time to get to know each other. Besides, he won't do anything to jeopardise his relationship with me. He wants this too much.'

He gestured between them, and Rosa liked the

way it made her feel, as if she had an equal say in what they were doing. 'And, if he is angry with you, I'll deal with it.'

The initial tide of anxiety that had washed over Rosa ebbed a little, to be replaced by a stirring of excitement which she hardly dared to acknowledge. Could she do this—go off with Luca while nobody else would know where they were, or what they were doing? It felt frightening. She remembered how she used to push herself to do scary things when she still thought she could earn her father's admiration, or simply his attention. Could she push herself to do this, when she knew it might anger him, even though Luca would let him know?

'Well?' Luca raised an eyebrow at her. 'Was it presumptuous of me to book a restaurant for lunch?'

The idea of being seen in a restaurant with a stranger was alarming but was also exciting. Besides, Luca no longer felt like a stranger to her. She'd spent longer with him and talked to him more than almost anyone else she could think of, outside her family and the staff at the palace. When he reached across the table and took her hand, she knew she'd throw caution to the winds of Palosia—because with her hand in his she could face her fears and she'd be safe.

CHAPTER ELEVEN

THE DOOR OF the low-slung car closed with a soft thud, and Luca strode around the front of it and slid in behind the wheel. He turned to look at Rosa, who was fumbling with the seatbelt.

'Allow me.' He took the buckle from her and clicked it into place. Then he reached into the door pocket and pulled out a leather case containing a pair of over-sized sunglasses.

'Yesterday afternoon, when I had the idea of taking you out, I bought these for you.'

'I already have sunglasses. They're in my bag.' She reached into her tote.

'Yes, I know you do, but these are about twice the size of yours, and one of the latest designer models.' He removed the glasses from their case, unfolded them and handed them to her.

'Oh...thank you. That was very kind, but why do I need extra-large sunglasses?'

'You'll see. Now, is your hat secure?'

'It will be, when I've undone my hair. Why?'

Rosabella pushed the sunglasses onto her face

and began to pull the butterfly pins from the loose bun at the back of her head. Luca turned away and busied himself with his own seatbelt as her fair hair began to fall over her shoulders like spun silk. He gripped the steering wheel in both hands and pushed himself back into his seat. At the touch of a button the engine came to life with a throbbing roar, then he reached for another button and the soft top of the car began to retract.

'This is why.'

He heard her soft gasp. 'Luca, no!' Rosabella's fingers curled around his forearm, gripping tightly.

'What is it?' He turned to look at her but her eyes were hidden behind the enormous dark lenses of the sunglasses. Was he taking this too fast? It was a lot to expect of her, but he was afraid she might lose her nerve and ask to go home if he gave her too much time to think about where she was and what they were doing.

He halted the retraction mechanism of the roof. 'It'll be okay, Rosa. I'll look after you.'

Her grip on his arm eased a little.

'Yes, I know you will,' she said, softly. 'But with the roof down I'd feel so...exposed.'

'Mmm. I understand why you feel that way but look at it like this...' He lifted her hand away from his arm but continued to hold it lightly. 'With the roof and the tinted windows closed, everyone is going to want to peer in to see who is hiding inside. If we let it down, very few people will give a second thought to the couple in it, sensibly protected from the sun by sunglasses and a hat. A few might look at the car, because it's unusual and powerful, but nobody will expect to see Rosabella, the sheltered princess of Palosia, in plain sight, and so they're unlikely to recognise you.'

He placed her hand in her lap and picked up her hat from the footwell, fitting it carefully onto her head. Her smooth forehead creased as she considered his words, and he could see indecision at war with determination in her expression.

Then she nodded. 'Okay. I suppose that could be true.' The tremor in her voice made his chest ache. He didn't want her to feel anxious or stressed. What should be an easy, fun excursion might be a massive ordeal for her. 'But…'

'But I promise that, if you aren't comfortable, we'll put the roof up again. You just have to say the word.'

He watched her face as he pressed the button again, seeing her jaw clench and her shoulders stiffen, but this time she didn't try to stop him. He eased the car into the stream of traffic as the roof folded itself away.

At the first set of red traffic lights, his theory was proved correct. A few passers-by glanced at the driver and his passenger before sliding covetous eyes over the sleek black body and silver trim of the car. When the lights changed to green, he pressed the accelerator and relished the deep roar of the engine and thrust of power as they pulled away from the surrounding traffic.

Soon they'd left the town behind them and were climbing up a switch-back road that swooped higher and higher up the mountainside, revealing spectacular views of valleys and the coastline with every turn. A warm breeze blew into their faces laden with the perfume of summer flowers. Sliding a sideways look at Rosa, he could see that she was smiling. He hoped that meant she was beginning to relax.

The restaurant he'd chosen was at the top of the mountain pass, with sweeping views down to where the sea churned against the rocks. Luca hit the button to kill the engine and at first silence descended on them, until the song of birds and the chirp of insects intruded on it. He unclipped his seatbelt and turned to face Rosa.

'Did you enjoy the ride?'

Her answer came in the form of the wide, spontaneous smile she gave so rarely. She nodded. 'Oh yes, I did. Thank you. It was unlike anything I've ever done before. I'm already looking forward to the drive down again.'

He laughed, tipping his head back against the

head rest. 'We'll go down a different way and then follow the coast road until we can cut back across the island to the royal estate.'

A smart *maître d'* welcomed them, and if he recognised Rosa he was too discreet to show it. He led them across the restaurant, weaving through tables of diners, out onto a stone terrace to a table in the corner. There were views up and down the coast, but their position was shaded and given privacy by a climbing rose that rambled over a wooden trellis above them. He handed them leather-bound menus and a wine list and rattled off a list of special dishes of the day.

Rosabella opened her menu but quickly snapped it closed again.

'Isn't there anything you'd like?' Luca berated himself silently. He should have tried to discover what she liked before presenting her with a complicated menu like this. He recalled how she'd pushed the food around her plate and hardly eaten anything at all at the palace lunch on the day they'd officially met. Perhaps she had very specific tastes, or even food intolerances.

'No, it's not that.' She shook her head. 'This may sound ridiculous to you, but I've never had to choose from a menu before. I have no idea where to begin. I'm sorry.'

Luca took the menu from her hands and placed

it on the table. 'It's I who should apologise. It was clumsy of me not to have realised that.'

Rosa removed her hat and shook out her hair. He reached out and took the hat from her and hung it on the back of a vacant chair.

'Thank you. Please don't apologise. You probably can't even begin to imagine how exciting and strange this is for me.' She glanced over her shoulder, along the terrace, as if to check that they hadn't been spotted or followed. 'It's strange, in a wonderful way, just to be here alone. It's liberating.'

Her voice dropped and she frowned. 'Having lunch at a restaurant may be an everyday thing for you, but it's the sort of normal thing which my father's rules have prevented me from doing. It's what he is so afraid of.'

The anger Luca felt every time he thought about how her life had been restricted, her experiences curtailed, coiled in his stomach again. His eyes fell on the collection of bright butterfly clips she'd pulled out of her hair and put in the pocket of her blouse. Rosa herself was like a beautiful, delicate butterfly trapped in a net, longing to find freedom in the sunshine and fresh air.

As they'd driven up the mountain the breeze had whipped warm colour into her cheeks, and her eyes shone, despite her frown. Suddenly Luca wished, very much, that he could set her free.

Their eyes met. 'You're not alone, Rosa. You're with me.'

Her lashes fluttered down to her cheeks. 'Alone with you, is what I meant,' she murmured the heat in her cheeks deepening.

'I want you to enjoy your day out, without thinking about your father. He's very afraid of losing control of you, just as you say he lost control of Sofia. He's made sure you're never exposed to temptation in case you give into it. He fears that a taste of freedom will become an appetite you can't suppress. And, talking of appetites, shall I order for both of us? You don't have to eat anything you don't like.'

Rosa loved it all, from the artisan bread dipped in superb local olive oil, to the delicate home-made pasta in a spicy sauce and the fresh strawberries served with bowls of thick cream and sugar to dip them in.

She ate with relish, having an appetite which felt sharpened by the fresh air and the sense of indulging in something slightly illicit. Was this how Sofia had felt when she'd abandoned Palosia and found Marco again? As if she'd cast off shackles and seized control of her own destiny?

Just for this one day, she wanted to enjoy how

it felt to be free. She had no doubt that, when her father heard Luca had taken her to a restaurant unchaperoned, he might forbid her from returning to the workshop for her scheduled day later in the week. Whatever Luca thought, King Fiero would not be willing to allow her to test the limits of her freedom without payback. Her days at the hat workshop were the highlight of the long weeks, especially during the winter when there was less to do in the garden.

Out here, at the top of the mountain, eating delicious food with Luca, she felt brave and invincible. She'd tried to obey the rules all her life, but the emotion swelling in her heart right now did not feel good or obedient. It felt like rebellion, and it felt empowering and glorious.

Except, confronting her father wouldn't be like this. Her stomach dropped at the idea of the interview she would have to have with him: the rage he'd fly into, the threats he'd issue. It would be frightening, and her father would use his skill with words to shred her determination, to cut her down to something small, worthless and as useless to him as she'd ever been. When she told him she refused to enter into a loveless marriage, he'd pour scorn on her romantic notions of love and demand to know where she thought she was going to find a man who might love her.

She had no illusions about that, and she'd tell

him so. She knew she would never find anyone to love her, but she'd rather live out her life on her own than be contracted to a man who married her for the wrong reasons—to satisfy greed or ambition, or to provide the heir her father needed.

But nothing he said, or did, could make her marry anyone. She had to find a way to sustain the bravery she felt now, until all this was over.

The thought that the day would soon end and she'd have to say goodbye to Luca tore at her heart. This day of freedom with Luca would be the day she looked back on all her life. His deep eyes seemed to see into her soul and his gentle touch set her nerve endings alight with a fire which burned to her core, melting any resistance she might have. These vivid memories would keep her going through darkness and despair, if necessary. She'd cherish them so that she could always remind herself of the joy to be found in the world in simple, every-day things.

She could not marry Luca, because he would never love her, but she'd never forget how he made her feel and would forever be grateful for the memories they were making on this day.

'Hey.'

Rosabella's attention snapped back to the present, where the warm breeze lifted the ends of her hair and the sun scattered diamonds on the sea below. The concern she saw in Luca's eyes made her heart squeeze. She smiled at him, grateful for it.

'Hey to you too.'

'Are you okay? This has been quite a day for you. Please tell me if you feel you've had enough of adventure, or when you'd like to go home.'

'Go home?' Surely he didn't believe she wasn't enjoying herself? 'No, not yet... I was just thinking.'

'I could see that.' His mouth did that little lift at one corner that she loved. 'Good thoughts?'

'Mostly. I'm trying to make sure I remember everything, so...'

Luca leaned back in his chair and his gaze on her face felt warm. 'Do you remember our meeting in the maze, twenty years ago?'

She smiled, surprised. 'A little, yes.' She traced a pattern with a fingertip in the condensation on her glass of iced water. 'I remember a boy—a boy who seemed very tall to me—being in trouble and lost and I showed him the way out.'

He leaned forward, resting his folded arms on the table. 'That was me.' His eyes held a deep intensity which she couldn't quite understand. 'I was in trouble because I was being taken to meet your father and I was going to be late.'

'You were being taken to meet your future father-in-law, you mean.'

He nodded. 'I was, but I didn't know that. Not then.'

'When did your father choose to tell you?'

Luca's mouth compressed and he turned his face away from her. She saw the grip of his hands tighten on his forearms before he dipped his head.

'He never did. I found out after he died—two weeks ago.'

Rosa felt her eyes fly wide. She'd assumed he would have known for as long as she had that their futures had been decided for them.

'But how is that possible? Why didn't he tell you? I've known for almost as long as I can remember, although I didn't know it was you.'

He was quiet for so long that she thought he wasn't going to answer at all. Perhaps this signalled the end of her glorious day out. He'd drive her home in silence with no explanation forthcoming. What had she said to annoy him so much? She shifted uncomfortably on her chair, wanting to leave, but then he took a long breath and looked up at her.

'My relationship with my father was not happy. He obsessively controlled every aspect of my life, and I rebelled against him. I thought I'd broken the hold he tried to have over me…'

'Luca, I'm sorry. You don't need to tell me this.'

'Yes, I do. You need to know about me. What I'm like. It'll make things easier for you.'

An urgency in his tone made her swallow her protest. She gripped her hands together in her lap.

'My father and I had barely spoken for a year, and before that all our exchanges had been angry. I'd left the family estate and carved out a career for myself, independent of him or my ancestry, and that infuriated him. I felt he was withholding something from me, which he planned to use against me at some time in the future. I assumed it was something to do with my inheritance.'

His smile was grim. 'When he died, I discovered how wrong I'd been. I found out I was engaged to a foreign princess from a country I barely remembered.'

Rosa needed to breathe but her lungs refused to expand beneath the weight she felt pressing on her chest. There was a buzzing in her ears, and she wondered, in an oddly detached way, if there was a swarm of bees passing by. When she heard Luca's voice again, it seemed to come from a distance.

'Rosa, are you alright?' She felt the touch of his hand on her arm, and thought fuzzily how good it felt, and then that she shouldn't get to like it too much because it couldn't last long. 'Rosa...?'

Finally, just as a shadow encroached at the edge

of her vision, she gasped, and much-needed oxygen reached her brain. She blinked. 'I'm sorry. I was shocked by what you said. I…'

Luca lifted her water glass and held it to her lips. 'Have some water. Just a sip. You're very pale.'

She shook her head. 'I'm usually pale. It's my complexion. It makes my freckles stand out.' Her words felt muddled. She inhaled another deep breath. Why had she mentioned her freckles?

'I've never noticed them until now, and I think they're beautiful. I'm sorry I had to shock you in order to see them.'

The tenderness in his voice was more than she'd ever heard, from anyone, before. Rosa took the glass from his fingers and swallowed a mouthful of water. 'I just assumed you'd always known. And to find out like that…it must have been shocking.'

'Did you ever wonder why I hadn't tried to communicate with you?'

'No. I was never given the chance to communicate with *you*. I thought you were…'

He arched an eyebrow, his gaze narrowing. 'What?'

'Mmm… I thought you must be like me. Bound to do your duty by your family.'

'I understand why you'd have been forced to accept your duty, especially after your sister defied your father's wishes. All his hopes for an heir now rest with you.'

She massaged her temples with the tips of her fingers. 'To escape my duty to my family and Palosia would be impossible. My life is here and the path I must take has never been in doubt. But...'

She was suddenly dangerously close to telling him that she would never marry him, but she pulled back. What if her admission angered him? He might insist on bringing the day of their marriage forward, to the earliest possible date, on her birthday. If he told her father, she'd be watched every moment of the day and night, in case she tried to run away, as Sofia had.

And yet she was sure Luca cared about her. She saw compassion and comprehension in his dark eyes, but she was not equipped to know if he was sincere. Her mother's warnings echoed in her head. He said he'd look after her, but how could she trust him? Her mother had believed her father's promises and declarations of love, but they'd all been conditional on her producing an heir.

For the first time ever, she questioned her mother's words. Her opinion of marriage had been formed by the way her husband had treated her and, like Rosa, she had no other experience with which to draw a comparison. But not all men were like her father. Sofia had found love with Marco and was ecstatically happy. Perhaps Luca was genuinely kind and considerate.

It felt as if a cloud had passed in front of the sun, dimming the brightness of this precious day, but when she turned her head she could see that the sea still sparkled and the waves still gleamed, foamy and white. She felt utterly confused, but amidst her confusion one thing stood out: more than anything, even if she never saw Luca again after today, she wanted to believe that he was trustworthy and honourable.

'I'm sorry I shocked you.' His voice was gentle. 'Can we not let it spoil the day?'

Luca felt her withdraw from him and it twisted his heart. Once again, he hadn't made allowances for the unnaturally sheltered upbringing she'd had. He should have anticipated how much his revelation would shock her, and he should have considered his words much more carefully.

He needed her to know what he was like. How he'd been taken from the loving home of his grandparents and returned to the castle in Tuscany without warning. How his stubborn determination not to be controlled had infuriated his father, led to bitter arguments and, eventually, estrangement from him. How he'd never known his mother and had always blamed his father for her death. If his mother had lived, perhaps his father would not have been able to arrange this marriage of convenience, or hide it for so long.

Watching Rosa across the table, and seeing the emotions shadowing her face, he wondered if his mother had fought an inner battle with herself, before deciding to defy her husband and ride that dangerous horse. And why, when she'd had a two-year-old son, had her duty to him not been stronger than her need to exert her own will? His grandparents had always insisted that she'd loved him dearly—but, if she'd loved him enough, surely she wouldn't have put herself in danger?

His father had got the heir he wanted, but had she been happy to accept her role of wife and new mother, her independence curtailed, her horizons narrowed? Perhaps she'd been unbearably frustrated and had rebelled against that as much as against the strict controls her husband had imposed on her.

Luca had always felt proud that he'd inherited his rebellious, independent spirit from his mother. King Fiero had gravely restricted Rosa's life, just as his father had tried to curtail his. Both had lost a young, beautiful wife for different reasons, and fear of losing more might have driven their subsequent behaviour.

Perhaps his father had imagined that, by binding his son to the marriage, he'd be securing himself against what the future might hold. He'd never know what had motivated the actions of either of his parents, but considering them from a different point of view made him feel uncertain, and his convictions not as unshakeable as they'd been until now.

He couldn't allow anything at all to interfere with his rock-solid opinion that the idea of this proposed marriage was the result of the greed and ambition of the two men who had brokered it. If Rosa understood how the events of his life had shaped him, perhaps she might understand the reasons why he could never marry her, and be less hurt by his abandonment.

Somehow, it had become important to him that he hurt her as little as possible. He'd watched her bloom over the past few hours like a beautiful, delicate flower unfurling its petals in the sun, and it had warmed his heart and touched him in a way he was reluctant to explore. What if he began to have feelings for her that went beyond not wanting to hurt her when he refused to marry her? What would he do about that?

The anxiety which had gripped her at the prospect of spending the afternoon with him, and possibly being recognised, had melted away and been replaced with openness and enjoyment. It was deeply rewarding to think he could make her happy and he wanted to keep her this way. He'd already been planning how to spend more time with her, but now he wondered if she'd agree to it. Her expression had become distant, and the smile to which he might just be becoming addicted had vanished.

A few petals drifted down to the table on the refreshing afternoon breeze from the rose-covered pergola above them. Luca picked one up and studied it. It was pale pink, darker at the edges, and smooth as satin. He rubbed it between his fingers, picking up its delicate, sweet perfume.

If he brushed his fingers across Rosabella's cheek, would her skin feel equally soft? He wanted to find out and his heart flipped as he imagined reaching across the table to touch her. The thought that she might recoil was what stopped him. He'd already demonstrated impaired judgement more than once today.

'When we met in the maze,' he said, finally catching her gaze again, 'You said you'd been named Rosabella because roses were your mother's favourite flower.'

In the silence that followed he felt as if she was weighing something up, and that her decision would be very important to him. He waited, giving her time, hoping to see the faint lines between her brows smooth away and a trace of her smile return. Her fingers which had been busy pleating the linen napkin stilled, and her face cleared. He released the breath he hadn't realised he was holding.

'Yes.' She nodded. 'I'm surprised you remember that.'

'Do you have a favourite flower?'

He thought she'd have a quick answer, but she glanced at him from beneath her lashes and shook her head. 'I think I do, but then I change my mind. There're so many to choose between, I never have a favourite for very long.'

'Well, then, what would your favourite be today?'

'Maybe roses? Because now they'll always remind me of…this. And you.'

'Even though I almost spoiled the day?'

She smiled, and his heart soared. 'I won't let anything, or anyone, spoil this day.'

CHAPTER TWELVE

MORE THAN ONCE on the drive back, Rosa slid a sideways look at Luca. His eyes were hidden behind dark shades, his mouth serious, with no hint of a lift at the corners. Since their conversation at lunch, he'd been quiet.

The road rose steadily through a series of twists and turns towards the hill on which the palace stood. Luca's hands on the wheel fascinated her. His strong fingers seemed to hold it lightly, but his touch was sure and decisive. The muscles of his thighs flexed beneath the denim of his jeans as he pressed the accelerator, releasing a burst of power and speed from the car.

Rosabella swallowed, her mouth dry, and shifted her gaze away from him to watch the countryside speed by the window. Why did watching his hands on the steering wheel make her remember their touch on her upper arms and wish she could feel it again? Or make her remember the feel of his rock-hard chest beneath her palms? If she put a hand on his thigh, how would it feel?

The gleaming palace came into view above them. Isolated from the outside world in the warm car, close to Luca, she wished the journey could continue for ever, but she knew she had to end it now.

'Luca?'

'Mmm?' He glanced across at her. 'Are you okay?'

'I'd like you to stop, please. There's a place just up ahead, next to a gate.'

'Sure.' He braked, slowing the car steadily, and pulled off the road, where a wooden gate was fitted into a gap in the wall.

As the throb of the engine died away on the still air, he unclipped his seatbelt and half-turned towards her, raising his eyebrows in a question.

'Care to tell me why? We'll be there in a few minutes.'

All at once his presence felt overwhelming. His shoulders blocked out the light. He shifted, flexing one knee and stretching an arm across the back of her seat.

'I...don't want to be seen arriving back with you.' She released the buckle of her own seatbelt and put a hand on the door, fighting the feeling that she wanted to stay here with him, cocooned in a world of their own. She needed to put more space between them before this pull that urged her to close the gap became too strong.

The way these unfamiliar feelings seemed to take control of her, threatening to allow her body to act against her better judgment, was frightening and confusing. Her mind knew exactly how she should behave but her body had developed a will of its own.

Luca regarded her in silence for a moment, before nodding. 'Okay, if that's what you'd like. I did send a message to your father, so he'll be expecting me to bring you back.'

She shook her head. 'It would still raise eyebrows and the staff would speculate. I'd rather avoid that.'

These memories needed to be kept safe, to belong to her alone. The idea of the gossip that would begin to circulate if it became known they'd spent hours together, unchaperoned, and how the facts would be picked over and discussed, made her angry.

Luca removed his sunglasses and dropped them into his shirt pocket, resting a forearm across the top of the steering wheel. His eyes were soft. 'Don't look so fierce.' He smiled. 'Where would you like me to drop you off? You shouldn't walk on the road. It wouldn't be safe, or seemly.'

Rosa tipped her head, indicating the gate. 'That

gate leads into the orchards. I can make my way from here up through the garden.'

He leaned forward. 'It looks as if it's locked.'

'Oh, it is, of course. But I know the combination.'

'Do you often let yourself in or out of it if you want to keep your movements secret?'

'No, of course not. I'd never...' She stopped, seeing the quirk of his mouth and the gleam in his eyes. 'Are you teasing me?'

'I am.' His smile sent heat barrelling through her, melting the barrier she'd been about to put up. Teasing was something new to her, and it felt fun and intimate. 'Except for today, when we definitely want to stay under the radar. And, just to keep things above board, I'm going to deliver you safely back into the garden. Nobody can object to that.'

Rosabella wished she could think of a light-hearted response, but her mind had stalled. 'Thank you,' she said. 'Nobody will see me... or us.'

'You're sure you'll be alright?'

'Yes.' Something inside her warmed at his concern. She turned her face towards him. 'Thank you, for the most wonderful day.'

He smiled, again, his eyes crinkling at the corners. 'When will you next be going to the factory?'

She ducked her head and pulled her tote and hat onto her knees.

'On Thursday—the day after tomorrow.'

'I've had a look at a map of Palosia and there's a beach I'd like to explore. It's remote but I think it's accessible. Will you come with me—on Thursday?'

'To the beach?' Rosa pressed a hand against the place in her abdomen where she felt the stirrings of panic.

'You said you like swimming.'

'I... I do. But I haven't swum in the sea for so long. I don't think...'

'You don't have to swim,' he murmured. 'Just be with me.'

'Won't you have gone by Thursday?'

He frowned, running a thumb along his jaw. 'I'll have to leave on Saturday. I'm booked on a flight from Rome to New York on Sunday.'

Something caught in her throat and she swallowed. The reality of the situation felt hard and unforgiving. He would leave on Saturday, and she would never see him again. He'd be furious to be rejected by a shy princess with no other prospects, but he'd soon find someone else, someone worldly and experienced, who could be the wife he needed.

'Well? What do you think, about the beach?'

The beach... She imagined the fine, white

sand tickling the soles of her feet and the azure of the water deepening to inky blue where it lay in the shadows of overhanging rocks. She could almost feel the push and pull of the waves, with their foamy crests.

Soon, her life would become...what? She'd had a taste of freedom and normality with Luca, but she knew it would never be repeated. She doubted she'd ever be allowed to leave Palosia, even to visit Sofia and Marco. She'd have to return to marking out the weeks with charity work, caring for her mother and helping to maintain the gardens.

It was difficult to remember that she'd been resigned to her future until she'd crashed into the hard wall of Luca's chest and he'd stopped her from falling.

She was falling, anyway—falling for him.

But she couldn't give those feelings the oxygen they needed to breathe or grow. She had to stifle them now. Even if she fell in love with Luca, she would not agree to the marriage because he would never be able to love her back. He would find being shackled to a woman to whom he was indifferent frustrating, and he'd want his freedom.

She accepted that she was unlovable. Just because a handsome, charming man had paid her attention for a few hours shouldn't make her doubt it. A loveless marriage was unthinkable. But a marriage in which she loved Luca and he didn't love her back would be much, much worse.

'What do you think?' His voice sounded rough, edgy.

Rosabella dragged her thoughts back to the man who sat so near to her and yet was so utterly out of her reach.

'What do I think?'

What would he say if she told him where her thoughts had been? There was no room for love in a marriage of convenience, and it wasn't necessary for him to spend time with her, even if he had asked for the opportunity for them to get to know each other. All he needed to do was agree on the formalities with her father, so was he simply being polite? She couldn't believe that he really *wanted* her company, but perhaps being with her was a convenient way to fill the time until he returned to New York.

'Yes. About the beach?'

Was it so wrong to want to feel that all-consuming security that his body provided again? Could anyone blame her for snatching a few hours of excitement? She thought of Sofia, and she knew exactly what she'd say if Rosa asked for her advice: *Yes! Go for it!*

'The beach sounds like a wonderful idea.'

'Good. I'm glad you think so. I'll inform your father that I'd like to take you out, again.'

Was he glad, or simply being kind? She wished she had some way of knowing.

'I must go.'

'Yes.'

But she didn't move. She could feel the warmth of his body so close to hers, and hear his steady breathing, a reassuring counterpoint to the way her own was becoming uneven and quick.

'Rosa, I...'

There was a new intensity in his voice and suddenly she was afraid of what he might say. If he'd changed his mind about the trip to the beach... She leaned forward to open the door but her shaking fingers slipped on the smooth metal of the handle.

Luca stretched across her. His forearm pressed against hers as he released the door easily. All her attention focussed on the place where their arms touched. His skin was tanned and smooth, against the fairness of hers, his arm corded with muscle. His hands and fingers looked strong and capable.

Capable of what? How would they feel, stroking over her face or body? The need to discover whether reality matched up to her imagination swelled inside her. She wanted to prolong the contact but that thought frightened her. If she turned, she could press her cheek against the crisp cotton of his shirt and inhale his scent of pine forests and citrus groves, which she could never quite get enough of when he was near.

Most of all, she could press her hands against him and feel that...*safety*. As if he'd always catch her when she fell, or that he'd never let her fall at all. His fingers lingered on the door handle and then brushed across her hand and arm with a feather-light touch as he moved away.

Her chest felt tight, and her heart thrummed against her ribs. She'd been thinking about his touch, longing for it, but afraid of the idea of it. Yet somehow, in the confined space of the car after the day they'd shared, the intimacy of the gesture didn't shock her. It felt normal and right.

If only the fear of rejection didn't stop her from acting on what her body wanted her to do.

Luca pushed the driver's door open and walked round to the passenger side.

The few seconds it took him were not nearly long enough. He needed minutes—scrub that, he needed days—to nail this down. He was practised at ordering his mind. It was an essential skill in his profession. And it was how he'd had the gritty determination to lead the life he wanted, not the one his father had decreed.

His body had always been biddable, so what

the hell was going on with it now? And what was it about Rosa that sent it into overdrive, out of control and rushing headlong towards disaster?

Was this going to prove to be his father's ultimate victory over him? The grim irony that he could end up wanting the one woman in the world he would never allow himself to have, because his father had chosen her, was not lost on him.

He pulled open the door. Rosabella swung her long legs out of the low car, clutching her tote and hat. Luca extended his hand and she took it. His fingers closed around hers as he helped her from the car, and he felt as if he could finally breathe out with relief because, at last, he was holding her hand. Then it seemed the most natural thing in the world for him to draw her close, brush his mouth against her temple in the lightest of kisses and hold her, briefly, against his side.

He wanted to pull her into his arms and feel her soft body relax and melt against the hot, hard planes of his. And then he wanted to wrap her hair around his hand, tip her head back and kiss her until neither of them could remember what day it was.

But he released her. He sucked in a long, steadying breath. These thoughts and feelings were inconvenient and impossible. And disrespectful. In a few days he'd be gone, having severed all ties with Palosia and its antiquated customs and restrictions—the ones in which his father had so deviously entangled him. There was no place for him in this world, or for Rosa and him in any world at all. He needed to get back to his own life, and quickly, hopefully without leaving too much damage in his wake.

What, in the name of all things sensible, had made him suggest taking Rosa to the beach? She was vulnerable and innocent, and the quicker he got out of her life, the better it would be for both of them. She needed care and gentleness—*commitment*—not the bitterness his upbringing had left in him, or his soul-deep distrust of the idea of love.

If his father had loved him, surely he would never have entangled him in this impossible web of obligation? If his mother had loved him, would she have gambled with her life when she must have known she might lose it? His grandparents: they hadn't had a choice. They'd had a bereft two-year-old thrust upon them with orders from his father to care for him, until he'd decided he wanted him back.

If he married Rosa, and they had a son, they'd be under pressure for the boy to be taken from them to be raised by King Fiero as his heir. Even if he wanted to marry her, he could never enter into an agreement which would put pressure on them to remove a child from its mother. He'd had the benefit of the love of his grandparents, but the wound left by the death of the mother he didn't remember remained raw.

Just as well, then, that the chances of him marrying her were significantly worse than a snowball's in hell. He should stop this—now.

But his eyes caught Rosa's and held, and he knew he wouldn't do that. Why deny her a little more pleasure? And why deny that he wanted to spend time with her? She was utterly different from any woman he'd ever met, and he found her beguiling and intriguing. When she was relaxed, she was delightful company—fresh and spontaneous—and he loved that he was able to give her that. And, when she looked stressed, he wanted to hold her and erase the worry from her beautiful face. Why was that wrong?

Because it was dangerous, his inner voice told him.

Her eyes were bright, her lips parted in surprise, and he wanted more than anything to cover them with his own and find out how sweet and warm she would taste. He took her hand again. 'I enjoyed the day too. Thank you.' He bent his head and kissed her fingers which were interlaced with his.

'Until Thursday.'

She turned abruptly, the late-afternoon sun

sparking golden highlights in her hair. He kept a hand hovering at the small of her back, his fingertips just brushing the waistband of her skirt as she punched numbers into a keypad on the gate post and disappeared through the gate. It slammed shut behind her.

For minutes he watched the place where she'd gone. Frustration at his inability to resist seeing her again made him thrust his fingers through his hair. He swore softly. He didn't understand this. He lived his life within certain rules and he was busy breaking them. When last had he ever not listened to the voice that told him to back off; that he was getting in too deep; that he might lose control of a situation?

His sense for detecting trouble was impeccable, but Rosa had scrambled it. He might have inherited his need for independence from his mother, but the iron grip he had on his emotions stemmed from the cold and unsympathetic upbringing of his father. The idea that he might not win this internal battle was unthinkable.

He slid back into the car and gunned the engine, revving it and pulling onto the road in a shower of gravel then turning downhill, away from the palace. The island roads, with their steep inclines and sudden bends, were perfect for indulging his love of speed and pushing his driving skills to the limit. He needed to focus on something immediate and taxing, away from the girl he'd come here to jilt.

He'd left Tuscany with the intention of dealing with this situation in a few hours. The only person he'd needed to meet with was King Fiero, but that plan had gone to hell from the moment he'd connected, literally, with Rosa. This should have been handled purely as a business transaction. He'd never made the basic error of allowing emotion to interfere with business.

Until now. A situation that should have been quick to resolve had turned into something much more complicated, in which desire was intent on sending the wrong messages to all the wrong parts of his body. He was playing with fire, but the pull of the heat was irresistible, and that was dangerous.

Danger could be addictive.

CHAPTER THIRTEEN

Rosa shaded her eyes and studied the beach. In the years before Sofia had first run away to try to find her mother, when the two of them had had freedom to explore their island home—although always accompanied by a member of the palace security detail—this beach had been a no-go area.

From above, it looked like a tiny piece of paradise. Gentle waves lapped at a perfect crescent of white sand and two rocky promontories curved out on either side, protecting the bay and keeping the water calm in most weathers. But the only way to reach it was to scramble down a steep slope, covered with boulders, thorny scrub and tall pine trees. The island abounded in beautiful, safe beaches and to risk breaking bones, trying to reach this one, was unnecessary.

But today they didn't need to scramble down to it because, when he'd collected Rosa from the factory, Luca drove to the tourist marina and hired a motorboat. They strolled along the jetty,

Rosa cautiously confident, after their previous outing, that her disguise of a floppy straw hat and big sunglasses would be effective.

The boat was sleek and powerful, with a canopy providing shade. Once they left the protection of the marina, Luca opened up the throttle and they bounced over the ruffled sea, with spray flying over the bows. Rosa laughed; she loved it. Luca seemed to be as skilled behind the wheel of a speedboat as he was behind the wheel of a car. After skimming over the sea for ten minutes, he cut back the speed and turned towards the coast.

Now she watched from the boulder he'd helped her climb onto while he made the boat secure. He'd pulled off his grey T-shirt, and his swimming shorts were slung low on his hips. His broad chest looked as solid as it had felt under her hands, and the way the defined muscles of his arms and shoulders flexed and stretched as he tied a mooring rope firmly around a rock made her clench her fingers and think about running her palms over them, exploring their shape and feel and adding them to her growing store of memories.

She'd never been even remotely close to this amount of beautiful, male skin and muscle. She envied the relaxed way in which he carried himself and how he seemed to be totally at ease and unselfconscious.

Rosa had changed into her modest one-piece

swimsuit in the factory bathroom, then had pulled her linen dress back on and tucked her underwear into her bag.

Not that she planned to get wet. The thought of stripping off her dress in front of Luca, even though her black one-piece was not at all revealing, made her cheeks flush hot and her heart lurch.

Luca jumped onto the rocks. 'Are you okay? Not seasick?'

She laughed, tipping her chin up to look at him. 'Not at all. That was so much fun.'

She followed him carefully until he jumped down onto the sand and held out a hand to her. Then somehow he continued to keep his fingers loosely linked with hers as they walked along the edge of the water, their shoulders bumping.

A thrill ran up her arm and down into her middle, making something in her stomach tighten and warm. Should she untangle her fingers from his and put more space between them, or should she leave them there, where she wanted them to be? What would he expect? She wished she knew how she should behave. She longed to appear carefree and relaxed but every cell in her body seemed to be on high alert and aware of the man next to her who swung her hand in his. Perhaps he'd simply forgotten to let go her fingers.

Luca stopped and crouched to smooth out a patch of sand and then pulled her down to sit beside him, releasing her hand. Even though his shoulder continued to brush hers, she felt bereft at the loss of the contact of his fingers as they sat, their feet in reach of the ripples that washed onto the beach, in an almost hypnotic rhythm.

She leaned back on her hands and buried her toes in the damp sand.

'Do you know this beach?' He bent up his legs and propped his elbows on his knees.

'I knew it was here, but it was dangerous to access it from the land, and I've never been on a boat.'

He turned to look at her, his dark brows drawn together. 'You've lived all your life on an island and you've never been on a boat?' He shook his head. 'If I'd known, I would have hired a bigger one. We could have gone further—taken a picnic.'

She pushed herself upright, dusting the sand from her hands and smiling. 'No. This is perfect. If we went further and returned too late, there'd be a search party out looking for me and I'd be in all sorts of trouble. And so would you.'

He shook his head, a dark lock of hair landing on his forehead. 'Not me. Surely it's acceptable to take the woman I'm—?'

'Luca.' She knew her voice sounded impeded and that he'd pick up on it. He seemed to be acutely attuned to her anxieties and insecurities.

'What is it?' He turned towards her, his eyes full of concern.

'Can we please not talk about that? This is such a beautiful place—so unspoilt.'

He raked his fingers through his hair, mussing it more than the wind on the boat had already done. 'And talking about the fact that we're supposed to marry each other will spoil it?'

Rosa pulled her bottom lip between her teeth, frowning, wishing she could be honest with him. But telling him now that she could never marry him would fracture this beautiful day into a million tiny pieces, and she wanted to keep it whole and perfect, to look back on in the future.

'Maybe.'

His narrow gaze was intense, locked onto hers. She tried to pull her gaze away and stare out to sea but the connection between them was too powerful. Her attention was dragged back to his, as if connected by an invisible thread which wouldn't allow her to look anywhere else.

He scooped up a handful of sand, fine as powder, and let it trickle through his fingers. 'If that's what you want, Rosie.' The gentleness in his voice reassured her. He wasn't going to insist on a discussion she didn't want to have. 'May I call you Rosie?'

The lump which formed in her throat stopped her from speaking, so she pressed a hand to her chest and nodded, despite thinking this was no time to start calling each other by familiar names. As soon as he discovered that she'd refuse to marry him, he need never think about her again. Her name would be scrubbed from his mind. From his *life*.

'Would you like to go in for a swim to cool off?' He stood up. 'Either that, or you need to find some shade. You must take care not to get sunburned.'

Rosa nodded, torn between wanting to be honest with him and not wanting to spoil the day with a confrontation. Already the easy atmosphere between them had become charged, and the sight of his tanned, sculpted chest and taut abdomen made her stomach clench and awareness prickle along her nerve-endings.

She dropped her gaze and began to walk along the edge of the water, treading carefully in the soft, wet sand, to where overhanging rocks cast some shade. It was very warm. Sweat trickled between her shoulder blades and pricked her scalp. She lifted her heavy hair off her neck and puffed out a breath, wishing she could be like Luca, unconcerned about baring her body, and could pull off her dress and plunge into the water. She watched as he waded in and then dived beneath the surface, shaking his head as he came up again, flicking his hair back so that a shower of drops arced through the air.

With a body like that, of course he wouldn't

mind others looking at it. He flashed a smile at her and raised a hand, and then he struck out, swimming across the bay with long, easy strokes, his powerful arms cutting cleanly through the water. It was years since she'd swum in the sea and the lure of it was strong. She could smell the saltiness of the water and almost taste it on her tongue.

Luca kept swimming until he reached the end of the headland. She watched him pull himself onto the rocks, shake water from his hair and stretch out on his back, his arms folded behind his head.

Perhaps he was far enough away for her to be safe for a few minutes. She'd watch carefully and leave the water as soon as he dived back in. She dropped her hat and sunglasses, grabbed the hem of her dress and tugged it over her head. Before she could over-think it, she ran into the water, letting the shallow waves swirl around her ankles, delighting in the refreshing coldness.

She waded in further until a larger swell brought the water over her knees, around her thighs. It was cold enough on her heated skin to make her gasp, despite the warm sun on her back. She dipped her hands into the sea and let the water run through her fingers, then she took a deep breath and dived in, twisting as she surfaced to float on her back. The sun was dazzling so she closed her eyes. It was sheer bliss, rocking in the gentle swell, supported by the water. She forgot about protecting her face from the sun, forgot about...

Abruptly, she pulled herself upright, planting her feet on the sand beneath her and looked up to check on Luca. He'd vanished. She scanned the rocks for a sign of him, and then the water, but found none.

Then with a splash, he emerged beside her. Rosabella stifled a scream of shock and wrapped her arms around her body. A swell caught her off-balance and she staggered backwards.

Luca's hands caught her shoulders. His grip was just as gentle and firm as she remembered. Her palms splayed out across his chest and, in some detached part of her brain, she thought how much better it was, being able to feel his naked skin beneath her fingers rather than through the fabric of his shirt.

She was close enough to see drops of water clinging to the fine, dark hair that roughened his chest, and an insane urge to drop her head and press her mouth to his skin ambushed her.

He held her steady, but then, instead of releasing her, he eased her towards him until his firm stomach and the long, hard muscles of his thighs pressed along the length of her body as he continued to hold her.

The sun sparkled on the surface of the water and she blinked up at him, dazed. His head dipped and her gaze slammed into his. If he let her go now, she'd slip beneath the surface, her limbs reduced to a shaking mass, but, if she stayed where she was, she would drown in the dark depths of his eyes that seemed to see what she wanted before she knew it herself.

Either way, she was doomed.

'Luca.' Was that *her* voice? It was husky with a need she didn't understand and wouldn't have been able to articulate.

'Mmm?'

She heard the rumble in his chest through her palms, because her ears were filled with the sound of his deep, steady breathing, the beat of her own heart and the rush of blood through her veins.

Dreamily, she moved her hands, searching for his heartbeat, curious to know if it was as wild as her own, and her palm brushed across the hard bead of a nipple.

His sudden, harsh intake of breath shocked her, and her head jerked back.

'I... I'm sorry. I didn't mean to hurt...'

One of his hands released her shoulder and slid to cover hers where it lay on his chest, pressing down. The other slipped across her shoulder blades and down to the small of her back, exerting a gentle pressure that eliminated any space left between them. She circled her free arm around his waist, astonished at how easy it was to make the movement.

'Don't be sorry, Rosie.' His voice had a ragged edge. 'You didn't hurt me. It's just...' His attention dropped to her mouth as he sucked in another sharp breath. 'It's just that I want... I *need*...to kiss you. But I'm so afraid of hurting you.'

'You won't hurt me, Luca.' She lifted her face towards him and saw a mix of confusion and conflict in his eyes. She wanted to resolve whatever internal battle he was engaged in, but mostly she wanted this to last for ever.

His glance moved up and fixed on hers. He lifted his hand and traced his index finger across her bottom lip and then shuddered as she opened her mouth and sucked on his fingertip.

'Dear God, Rosie,' he breathed, tipping her chin up with his finger, and she could feel the moistness from her mouth on its tip. 'I shouldn't do this. It's not...'

'Luca, please. I want you... I *need* you...to kiss me.' She rose onto her toes, dragging her body against his, feeling every muscle in him tense beneath her touch. He coiled her braided hair around his hand and gently eased her head back, his gaze fused with hers.

'Rosie, are you sure?' His voice was a whisper against her lips.

'Yes. Oh, yes.'

As his mouth finally found hers, sensation swamped everything else. His kiss was tentative, then firm but gentle. He eased away from her for a moment, pressing his lips to her forehead, but she reached up and buried her fingers in his hair, pulling him down again. He breathed in, his chest expanding against hers and then he claimed her again, his mouth moving restlessly, easing her lips apart to allow his tongue to stroke against hers.

Rosa felt as if she'd finally found something she'd been searching for all her life. As if everything she'd ever done, every thought she'd ever had, had been leading up to this moment. As if she'd found home and never wanted to leave its safety again.

And yet it also felt shockingly new, unbearably exciting and erotic, and her body screamed for more, although more of what she didn't know. She just wanted this not to stop; to see where it would take them both.

How was it possible, she wondered in the last lucid moment before a surge of need and white-hot physical desire swept her away, to feel so completely safe in the arms of this rock of a man, yet at the same time teeter on the edge of something terrifying and dangerous?

CHAPTER FOURTEEN

HE HADN'T MEANT to kiss her. It was wrong and he needed to stop. Perhaps he could have, if the communication between his brain and his body hadn't malfunctioned. But who was he kidding? Somone had pressed 'override' and that someone was him.

Rosa tasted just as sweet and warm as he'd imagined she would, since that moment when their bodies had collided and he'd held her briefly against him. Because it was no use pretending he hadn't thought about it every time he'd seen her and most of the time when he hadn't.

He'd persuaded himself that he wanted to get to know her better so that he could explain to her, in as reasonable and gentle a way as possible, that he could never marry her. And he did want that. She deserved to be treated with care and respect. Her father had agreed with his suggestion with scepticism, no doubt thinking that it was easier to humour him than to object. Luckily her father couldn't see him now.

He wanted to make sure she'd be alright when he left her. But he wanted this so much more. The hot sun, the dazzling light on the sea and the cold water seemed to have induced a kind of madness in him. He felt driven by a need simply to be here with her, in this moment.

He felt as if he'd known her all his life. He smiled against her mouth at that thought. Technically, he'd known her since he'd been thirteen years old. Imagining her in his arms, her mouth beneath his and more, had been the subject of his waking and sleeping dreams for days.

She should have *stayed* in his imagination, but even as he acknowledged the folly of what he was doing he knew that, whatever happened in the next few minutes, days, or the rest of his life, he would never regret this.

She was warm and soft, her arms around him taut, her legs against his thighs long and lean. Her fingertips trailed over his back, straying innocently into the zone at the base of his spine, which sent a charge of electricity to his groin.

He tried to suppress a groan, but knew he'd failed when her whole body tensed against his, her hands came up to bury themselves in his hair and she began to kiss him back with an unpractised, wild fervour that threatened to part him from every last vestige of his shredded self-control. She swayed against him as the sea swirled around them and on the next swell he slid his hands behind her thighs and lifted her, so that her chest was pressed against his and her legs wrapped around his waist.

The contact, the friction, between them was building to beyond bearable and he sank to his knees. She gasped against his mouth as the cold water lapped at their shoulders.

With a monumental effort, Luca pulled his mouth from hers and cupped her face in his hands. 'You're cold. I'm sorry...'

She shook her head. 'No. I'm so warm, against you.' She pressed closer to him and then lightly licked along his jaw, making him clamp it beneath her tongue. 'And you taste so good.'

He tightened his arms around her. 'Try to be still, Rosa.' His voice hissed through his clenched teeth. He rested his forehead against hers, his chest heaving as he fought for control.

She pulled back her head and he saw the focus returning to her wild eyes. Her arms slid from around his neck and her hands came to rest on his chest. Her gaze dropped.

'Luca, I'm sorry. I'm doing this all wrong. But I...'

His heart squeezed as she shook her head, avoiding his eyes. 'No, no, you're not. Rosa, look at me. *Look at me.*'

But she shook her head again. He slipped his

hands into her hair and drew her towards him, cradling her head in the place where his neck met his shoulder. She began to shiver. Holding her tightly against him, Luca stood and carried her out of the sea. He gently allowed her body to slide down his until her feet touched the sand.

'I'm sorry,' she said again. 'I should never have...'

He kept holding her against his chest and circled his other arm around her waist, holding her firmly. He dropped his cheek to rest on the top of her head.

'You should never have...what?' He turned his head and kissed her hair. 'Come to the beach with me? Gone swimming?' He took her hands, drawing them up to his chest.

'All of those things. But mostly I shouldn't have kissed you.'

'I was under the impression that I kissed you first.'

'But I kissed you back.'

'Mmm. You did.'

'And I did it all wrong, so you wanted to stop.'

'It was I who was in the wrong. I shouldn't have kissed you. I wasn't going to but—'

'But I threw myself at you.'

She looked stung, hurt and crushed, and she turned away from him, brushing her fingers across her eyes.

'Rosie, it's not like that. Listen to me.' He reached out and circled his fingers around her wrist. 'Please.'

She pulled away from him, but she stopped walking away, digging her feet into the sand and wrapping her arms around her body. Her body, which had fitted so perfectly against his own that it felt as if they'd been cast in moulds to match each other. He'd felt the hard peaks of her breasts through the fabric of her swimsuit, and the restless shift of her thighs around his waist had almost driven him over the brink.

This was wrong, and torturous. He'd tantalised her, while fighting his body to prevent them from going any further. He'd always considered himself a match for temptation; he'd always been able to walk away from it. He still could, he told himself, but this was way more difficult than anything he'd ever had to do before. This would mean hurting someone. And hurting someone whom he realised he cared about more deeply than was safe or sane.

'What?' Her voice trembled. 'What more is there to say?' She scrubbed at her face with the heels of her hands. 'I just feel so...*ashamed*.'

From the way she'd responded to him, Luca had no doubt that she'd never been kissed before, and now he needed to make sure that she didn't look back on it as something shameful or secretive. He inhaled deeply, steadying himself, because he needed to hold her and reassure her, but his body wouldn't want to stop at that.

Stepping behind her, he put his arms around her waist. The top of her head fitted perfectly beneath his chin.

'Wanting to kiss someone is nothing to be ashamed of, Rosie. It's a way of expressing your feelings when you can't find the words. It's a way of communicating with actions.'

She turned her head and pressed her cheek to his chest. 'I wanted to kiss you. But you wanted to stop. And I feel ashamed, because I wanted more and you didn't.'

'I wanted to kiss you, too. And I didn't want to stop, Rosie.'

She twisted in his arms, backing away, pressing her hands against his chest. Her eyes were shiny.

'Please, Luca, don't lie to me. I can bear most things, but I don't want to have to bear that. Be honest with me, even if the truth hurts.'

He reached out and brushed away a tear that had escaped with the pad of his thumb, afraid that his touch might send her running from him. She flinched but she didn't pull away.

'Why,' he asked, cupping her cheek in his palm, 'Would you think I'm lying? I didn't want to stop, but if we hadn't stopped then I wouldn't have been able to.'

He waited, watching her eyes dip and rise to his face again, her teeth catching her lip and releasing it, her chest lifting in a shaky breath.

'I don't believe you,' she eventually said, her voice barely above a whisper. 'Because nobody will ever want to kiss me, so why should you?'

If this was how a mix of fury and compassion felt, he didn't like it. It was confusing as hell. He wanted to punch something, or preferably someone, but at the same time he wanted to focus all his energy on making her feel safe and desirable. *Lovable*.

'Who,' he asked, fighting to keep his voice level, 'Has made you believe that about yourself? Because it's so far from the truth, it'd be laughable if it wasn't so cruel.'

Knowing that pulling her close would catapult him straight back into the danger zone, but not caring, he slid his hands down her sides, feeling her shiver as his fingers traced over her rib cage, then wrapped her in a tight embrace.

'I've always known I'm not lovable, Luca,' she said into his chest. 'My father has always made that clear. That's why he arranged for me to marry you. He said I should be grateful he'd found a husband for me.'

'Believe me, Rosa, that is criminally untrue.

You're beautiful, kind, gentle and generous. Men would be lining up to marry you in their dozens, if your father hadn't kept you under such insane control. My own father was a greedy, ambitious man who saw our marriage as a way to advance his status as a member of a royal family.'

He adjusted his arms around her, settling her closer. 'Along with you, your father gave him several vineyards which adjoin what is now my estate in Tuscany, increasing its value enormously—and to seal the deal an emerald mine in Brazil, on the birth of a son.' He tried to keep distaste out of his tone.

Rosa tipped up her head, squinting into the sun. He lifted a hand and shielded her eyes from the glare.

'He's giving so much away. What's he getting in return for me?'

Luca smoothed a hand over her hair, tucking a stray curl behind her ear. He took his time, choosing his words carefully.

'There've only been boys born in my family for generations. It's no accident that King Fiero sought out the Montenale name when he decided to secure his lineage. The promise of a son is all he wants—our son.'

CHAPTER FIFTEEN

LUCA RETRIEVED HER things from the shade and Rosa put on her hat and sunglasses. She pulled the silk ribbon, crusty with dried salt, from the end of her braid and Luca helped her to unravel her damp hair. He brushed his fingers through it, spreading it over her shoulders and down her back.

She knew it would dry in unruly curls and waves, guaranteed to give Luisa a headache if she saw it, but that felt trivial. They sat on the sand until her swimsuit was dry enough for her to pull on her dress again, and then they walked along the beach to the boat.

The return journey held none of the fun Rosa had felt earlier. The breeze had freshened, whipping up waves that lifted the boat then dropped it with a thud into troughs. Rosa clung to her seat, feeling cold and slightly ill. She shivered.

Luca lifted a hand from the wheel and reached for the towel he'd used earlier to brush sand from his body. He dropped it over her shoulders, then quickly took control of the boat again as it lurched over another wave. She gripped the towel in her fists under her chin, grateful for the protection it gave from the sharp wind.

Luca, she thought, had to be one of the most thoughtful and kind people she'd ever met. It was difficult to remember that he was also the tough, ruthless lawyer who fought tirelessly for the rights of his clients. And that he'd come to Palosia to discuss the business details of their marriage deal.

Had her father ever treated either of his wives with this sort of care and attention? She supposed he must have, in the early days of courtship and marriage. She knew her mother had been overwhelmed by his extravagant gifts and promises.

Promises and gifts were easy to give. But the way Luca paid quiet attention to her, and took notice of her needs almost before she was aware of them herself, was a much rarer and more precious thing.

If she ever fell in love, it would be with someone who had similar qualities of gentleness, kindness and quiet strength. Someone who made her feel safe and protected enough to allow her to explore her own strengths and desires, knowing he'd always be ready to catch her if she fell. Nothing could be further from the cold, businesslike arrangement her father had committed her to.

In her heart she wanted to believe Luca's kind, sweet words, because she desperately wanted him to be an honourable and honest man. But, even on a sun-kissed day at the beach, his words couldn't wipe away the years of her father's negative opinions, and her mother's insistence that she should never, ever trust a man.

Were his words simply an example of what her mother meant? He'd gain wealth and prestige by marrying her. If she'd listened to her head, she would have maintained the aloof attitude she'd adopted when they'd met in her father's antechamber. She'd have refused to walk with him in the garden or show him around the hat factory. Most of all, she would have turned down this trip to the beach, which had led her to behave in such a shameful way.

But if she hadn't agreed to spend time with him… Her heart squeezed at the thought. If she'd stayed in her rooms, refused to meet him… No, she didn't want to begin to imagine that scenario. Because if she'd hidden herself away, refused to get to know him even a little, she'd have been denied the memories of these precious and incandescent hours together.

Her freedom could be limited, her life made lonely and bleak, but no-one could steal her memories. Even though her heart felt in danger, she was glad she'd listened to it. That knowledge gave her a feeling of quiet strength.

Rosa was glad to reach the privacy of Luca's car. They'd returned the boat to the marina and walked back along the jetty, but she felt stressed. It was probably just her over-active imagination that made her think heads turned in their direction, eyes speculative as comments were made behind hands. It was because she felt embarrassed and ashamed, despite Luca's attempts to reassure her. She convinced herself of that.

She climbed into the car and sank into the comfort of the leather seat. Luca stared straight ahead as he started the engine and she tried to look anywhere but at his lovely, strong hands gripping the wheel or releasing the handbrake, so close to her thigh. Watching his hands would only make her remember how they'd felt on her body, or cupping her face, and make her wonder how she was ever going to get used to having to live without those sweet sensations.

Without him.

To her relief, he did not suggest lowering the roof. She wanted to hide behind the tinted windows. And she wanted to hide from him.

What must he think of her? She cringed. She wanted the journey to be over. She wanted this pain to end. Because she knew when she exited the car she'd be saying goodbye to him. It was no use to think otherwise. Tomorrow she'd request a meeting with her father and change the course of her life, for ever. Every moment she spent with Luca now simply prolonged the agony of knowing that she wanted to be with him but could never agree to marry him.

She was lost in her thoughts when he braked and pulled the car off the road.

'I thought you'd probably want to go back through the gate again.' He nodded towards the locked gate in the stone wall.

'Oh. I...yes, I suppose so.' She reached for the door handle, but he put out a hand and took her fingers in his.

'Rosie.'

She didn't want to look at him but found she couldn't look anywhere else. His eyes, dark with some emotion she wasn't equipped to understand, caught hers and held them.

'I should go.'

He nodded. 'Do you have a phone?'

Surprised by his question, she stumbled over her words. 'Yes, but it's not much use. Anyway, why do you want to know?'

He shook his head. 'I suppose I just want to know that I can contact you.' He ran the pad of his thumb across her knuckles. 'Do you mind if I look at it?'

Rosa dug in her tote, under her underwear, to find her phone. It felt as though changing into her swimsuit at the factory had happened in another life. She held out the phone to Luca.

His brows drew together. 'That is your phone?' He didn't take it from her. 'If you'd rather not...'

'I don't mind.' She shrugged. 'It's very basic, I know. It can only make and receive calls and texts. It's not "smart".'

He took the phone from her and turned it over in his hands. 'Do you have any access to the Internet?'

'No, although it's been available on Palosia for years. And I know that this phone is not secure. After my sister ran away, my father made sure of that. I didn't have a phone at all for a while. Then I was given this one. I don't use it much. I'm sure all my calls and messages are monitored. My sister phones me on it sometimes. That's the best thing about it.'

'Right.' He nodded. 'Do you mind if I take your number?'

'Why do you want it?'

'Because I'd feel better if I know I can contact you, even if everyone else knows about it before you do.'

'Okay. I don't really like to use it, apart from the calls from Sofia. It's just a reminder that very little about my life is my own.'

Luca was silent, but he pulled out his own phone and entered her details into it.

'Thank you.'

She shoved the phone back into her bag. 'Now...'

'Just in case you're thinking otherwise, Rosie,

I've loved being with you. I want you to know that. I don't want you to feel embarrassed, or ashamed or any of those negative things. You're beautiful, and *today* was your own.'

Hearing him say those words did something to her, as if he'd read her mind and understood about the memories. Suddenly, she wanted to show him that she'd do her best to banish the negative thoughts and beliefs that had been ingrained in her for so long. She felt a surge of that inner strength she'd unearthed.

'Then will you do something for me?'

'Anything in my power, yes.'

'Will you drive me back to the palace, to the main, big entrance door? I'm tired of being the obedient princess who always follows the rules and does as she's told. I don't care who sees us, or what they think.'

The words sounded braver than she felt, but it was too late to rethink them or take them back. Luca stared at her for a moment, then one corner of his mouth tugged upwards, and it was all she could do not to put out her hand, cup his jaw and touch her thumb to his quirked lip.

'Absolutely, Rosie. And I will handle any fallout we receive when we turn up unexpectedly together.'

She shook her head. 'No. *I* will.'

The tug at his mouth turned into his devastating, full-blown smile. He pressed the ignition button and eased the car onto the twisty road, heading up the hill towards the palace.

They stopped in a shower of gravel under the palace portico. The huge oak door, studded with metal, was closed and the forecourt was deserted. Luca strolled round the bonnet of the car and pulled open her door, taking her hand to help her out.

She swung her bag over her shoulder. 'Thank you.' She felt the tremor in her voice but hoped he couldn't hear it. She would walk away as if she expected to see him again, even though it felt as if something was tearing her heart apart.

He leaned forward to kiss her cheek. 'Thank...'

Behind them the door crashed open. Her father stood framed in it for a long few seconds, and then strode towards them, one of his secretaries hurrying in his wake.

'I don't need to ask where you've been,' he thundered, thrusting a mobile phone in front of Rosa's face. 'Because I can see for myself, along with the rest of the world.'

All the moisture left Rosa's mouth and her twisted heart suddenly beat painfully in her throat. She removed her sunglasses and looked at the phone. On the screen was a photo of Luca and her, walking along the jetty at the marina. Her bag swung from her shoulder, her hat shaded her face and her sunglasses hid her eyes. Luca was beside her, carrying a small backpack, his shorts and grey tee-shirt not hiding any details of his built physique. His head was bent towards her. There was no mistaking their identities.

Is this the man the King is forcing our Princess to marry? Shouldn't she have a say in the matter? the caption screamed.

There were already hundreds of likes and comments.

She tried to swallow past the dryness, trying to find her breath. She felt exposed, stripped of the unique feeling of safety being with Luca gave her. An echo of the words he'd spoken, in his deep, reassuring voice, hammered in her head: *today was your own.*

Today was suddenly tarnished. Luca's reassurance had strengthened her fragile self-belief. His words had given her the courage to return to the palace openly with him, ready to face her father and tell him of her decision.

The day which had been her own—*their own*—was no longer something she'd be able to revisit in her memory, delighting in the wonderment of being in Luca's arms, tasting the salt on his skin, feeling his lips on hers and his strong, insistent heartbeat under her palm.

Someone had recognised her and snapped her picture then shared it with hundreds, possibly thousands, of others who would now be picking over every detail and expressing their opinions on it. Moreover, the caption would add fuel to the embers of the fire of the succession debate, which only needed something like this to fan it into a little flame that might then flare up into a bigger, much more dangerous blaze.

The people of Palosia loved Queen Chiara and disagreed with the way the King treated her. She'd worked tirelessly for the poor of the island, setting up charities for women's education and employment. The hat business was one of her great achievements, but there were others. She'd established beautiful, open spaces where everyday citizens could relax in safety, and a botanical garden that was fast becoming internationally renowned for its collection of the flora that it protected, unique to the island.

The fact that she was unable to have more children was widely known, and sympathy for her ran deep. It was said that, if the King divorced her and married again in his quest for an heir, there would be a groundswell of outrage that might result in his removal from the throne.

He'd moved Queen Chiara and Rosa to a remote part of the palace and had never denied the rumour that he might end his marriage. That threat, unspoken though it was, had kept Rosa in line, obeying her father to protect her mother.

All these thoughts flashed through Rosa's

mind as she stood, frozen, staring at the picture on her father's phone. What if this was the spark that would reignite the debate about the succession only going through the male line? What if the rumble of dissatisfaction with the King's rule and his autocratic treatment of his family became a roar? Would it all be her fault?

'Rosie.' Luca's voice in her ear was low and steady and his use of the name that only he had ever used melted a little of the iciness inside her. The warmth of his hand on her arm sent a current of energy through her. 'It'll be okay. You're strong enough,' he murmured.

Luca was right, she thought, but he'd *made* her strong enough, with his kind words and encouragement. She could choose to believe her heart, that he was honourable and truthful. He made her feel worthwhile, as if she counted for something more than she'd always believed—and surely only the truth could make her feel the surge of strength and power she felt flowing through her now? Her fearful heart regained something closer to its normal rhythm and swelled with gratitude and another deep, unfathomable emotion. She raised her chin and met her father's furious gaze.

'What have you got to say about this?' The King's voice was lower, but no less angry. His eyes bored into hers and he swiped at the phone screen. Rosa saw there were other pictures, of the two of them boarding the boat and heading out of the marina, and then of their return, windswept and damp, with her hair a tangled mass.

Rosa returned his stare with an unwavering one of her own. If she saw a flicker of uncertainty cross his face, it was gone in an instant. 'I will not speak to you while you're so angry. Let me know when your temper has cooled. I will have something to say then.'

'How dare you defy me?' His voice rose again. 'What made you think you could disappear for hours on a boat, with a man you scarcely know? Answer me now.'

'Possibly the very same sentiment which made you think you could make me marry him. The boat trip lasted a few hours. Marrying him would be for life.'

Summoning all her strength and courage, Rosa walked past her father and away from Luca. The brush of his hand on the small of her back gave her the impetus she needed to keep going, through the door and into the hushed, cool palace.

Luca turned to face the King. He folded his arms across his chest and regarded the other man steadily from his superior height, waiting for him to speak.

The King's breathing was laboured in the silence, and he seemed to fight to control it.

'You, Montenale,' he rasped, 'Have treated me and my family with disrespect. I expected better of my future son-in-law.'

Luca raised a brow. 'In what way have I disrespected you, Your Majesty?'

The King huffed. As Luca had thought, he was not accustomed to having to explain himself. In a court of law, he'd have been able to pulverise the man's arguments in a few sentences.

'You said you wanted to take her out for lunch, but instead you disappeared with her in a boat.'

'That is correct, but I consulted with the princess beforehand, and it was done with her permission.'

'*Her* permission? She doesn't get to make decisions about what she can and cannot do. *I* make them. *Always.*'

Luca shook his head. 'Apparently not. She is perfectly able to make her own decisions.'

'This is the result of your influence.' King Fiero tapped the phone. 'Behaving like a woman with no morals, putting ideas into her head about independence.'

'I can assure you that Princess Rosabella does not need me to put ideas into her head. She has a plentiful supply of her own.'

The King's eyes bulged with anger. 'When she's your wife and she tries to assert her will, you'll think differently.'

Luca raked his fingers through his hair, rocking back on his heels. 'Contrary to what you believe, I didn't come to Palosia to claim the princess to whom I've been in an engagement of convenience for the past twenty years. When I discovered the existence of the agreement my father made with you, I was astounded that such a thing could be thought fit in the twenty-first century. On consideration, I recalled my father's antiquated and intransigent opinions regarding the liberation of women, and on meeting you I quickly realised he'd found someone who shared his views. Or, rather, I think you found him. The propensity of the Montenale line to produce male children is well known.'

King Fiero opened his mouth to interrupt but Luca held up a hand. 'We have a meeting scheduled for tomorrow morning. I'll be leaving Palosia on Saturday.' He bowed his head. 'Thank you.'

Luca got into his car and took his leave. When he glanced in the rearview mirror as he took the first bend in the driveway, a little too quickly, the King still stood where he'd left him, staring after the car. The temptation to fling in the man's face the fact that he could tear up the marriage agreement had almost shredded his control but, faced with his rage, he'd known that Rosa must hear his reasoning from him, not some twisted version the King might invent. He had to tell her first.

He exhaled heavily. He would head up into the mountains on the far side of the valley to find one of the hiking trails marked on his map. Then he'd go for a punishing run. The reserves of self-control he'd been forced to tap into to resist Rosie had proved to be only just deep enough, and his body still ached with frustration. The longing, the nameless *need*, to make them part of each other was all-consuming. If she hadn't stopped kissing him, thinking it wasn't what he wanted, he believed the thread of control that had been stretched tight would have snapped.

He had to pound all those thoughts and needs out of his mind and body so that he could meet King Fiero tomorrow with all his attention focussed where it needed to be. It was not going to be an easy or pleasant discussion. He would have to have all his wits about him, and have his negotiating skills at their sharpest, without his thoughts wandering to places to where he needed to forbid them from going.

But first, this evening, he had to see Rosie again one last time.

CHAPTER SIXTEEN

THE WALK THROUGH the palace to her rooms was a familiar route along marbled passages and colonnades, past courtyards where fountains played and ferns grew in cool, green shade.

Rosa frowned, bewildered. How could everything be so unchanged? All the familiar rugs, pictures and ornaments looked just as they had all her life—and yet she felt they should have taken on new shapes and colours, and the distances should have grown or shrunk, because she saw them through new eyes, experiencing them from a changed perspective.

The feeling that she hadn't been able to identify, but which filled her up so completely it had left no space for fear of her father or trepidation about the confrontation she needed to have with him, suddenly revealed its nature to her. The touch of Luca's hand, his words of encouragement and belief in her ear, had opened her eyes on a new world.

She loved him. She loved him, but she could

never marry him, because he didn't love her. Uniting their two families would grant him lands, riches and a royal wife, and all he would have to do was make sure he gave her a son.

What a sweet deal it was for the Count Luca Montenale. Why would he think he had to do anything more? Bringing love into the equation wouldn't enter his head. He was wealthy, successful, revered in his profession and stupidly handsome. Love was just a word to be bandied about, just a feeling that could not be described or pinned down. He'd have no use for that.

And yet she loved him for the way he'd made her feel: safe, interesting and cherished. And for the way he'd given her the strength and courage she needed to confront her father—to tell him that she refused to marry the man she loved.

How could she bear to do that now? She knew he was the only man she would ever love, and yet tomorrow she would deny herself the chance of being with him. She'd need all her courage. The thought that she might give in to her feelings and agree to her father's demands and Luca's expectations scared her. What irony that she must now use the courage he'd given her to tear herself from him for ever.

The passion and longing their kiss had unleashed in her felt unfathomable. The way Luca had held her, caressed her and claimed her mouth with a fervour that had felt almost desperate, made her want to believe he had found it as earth-shattering as she had. Yet that could not be true because she knew in her heart he could never love her.

How could he, when she was unlovable? What if trusting her heart had been the wrong choice to make? What if she gave in to these feelings, agreed to the marriage, to be with him, and then found her head had been right all along and he was only in it for what he'd get out of it? To love him and not receive his love in return would destroy her.

By the time she reached her quarters she thought she might be sick from the pounding in her head and the flood of emotions that confused and frightened her. Guilt at how she'd behaved with him in the sea, a longing to feel safe in his arms, grief that she never would again and anger towards her father for his egotistical belief that he could manipulate her life in this way all fought for her attention and threatened to drown her.

She paced the floor, then stopped at the window. It was early evening, and the heat faded as the light drained from the sky. The distant mountain peaks glowed pink in the setting sun. She turned away, unwilling to witness the beauty of nature when she felt as if part of her was dying. She buried her face in her hands.

Then she raised her head, straightened her spine and took a deep breath. She was not dying.

This would not defeat her. She couldn't let it. There was work to do with her mother's charities and in the garden, and nobody would ever know that her heart had been broken. She wouldn't allow anyone to have that satisfaction.

There was only one person in the world she wished she could talk to, and that was Sofia, but she strongly suspected that her conversations and messages were intercepted. She wasn't going to open her heart to Sofia, only to have others listening in and reporting back to her father. Anyway, Sofia and Marco would have seen the picture on the Internet by now, just as her father and thousands of other people had.

She copied Sophia's number into her address book, then switched the phone off and put it in a drawer in her bureau, deciding to let it run out of battery and never use it again. It would be better to have no phone than to worry about it being hacked if she used it.

She took a hot shower, sluicing away the sand and salt that still lingered on her skin and washing it out of her hair. Then she sat on her balcony and ate some of the supper Luisa had brought her, thankfully without asking any questions. There was no doubt that news of the confrontation she'd had with the King would have reached every last person in the palace by now. Speculation on it, and the social media debacle, would be rife.

Pink, violet and indigo infused the sky and the pale slice of a crescent moon rose over the mountains. Scents of lavender and roses wafted up on the warm evening air and Rosa knew that the one place she would find solace was in the garden. Pulling a cashmere pashmina around her shoulders for when the temperature cooled, she made her way quietly to the French windows and let herself out into the courtyard.

As she slipped under the archway she paused and glanced back at the palace. A handful of windows glowed with light but the only sounds came from the garden: the soft hoot of an owl, a mouse rustling in the border and the distant trickle of water.

Luca had returned hot and tired from his run but not feeling better in any way. The prospect of escaping from Palosia and returning to his normal life should have lifted his spirits, but instead it filled him with an unfamiliar kind of sadness.

He had to speak to Rosie. Before he saw her father, he wanted to tell her the truth. He owed her that. A rush of emotion had almost floored him when he'd listened to the firm, calm way she'd addressed the King. Her response had taken courage and determination. He knew she had both, and now he also knew she was not afraid to use them. At what had been a moment of extreme vulnerability, she'd dug deep and not capitulated to her father's anger and attempted bullying.

He felt proud of her and humbled by her bravery. It was more than pride, but he couldn't allow himself to admit to what he truly felt. It was safer to keep it hidden, even from himself.

Now he stood at his window and wondered how he could find her. He'd wanted her phone number because the idea of not being able to contact her had triggered a feeling of panic in his chest. She'd warned him that her phone was insecure, and he wasn't about to advertise to whoever it was on the King's staff who listened in to private conversations that he wanted to see her.

He could ring for the man who'd been assigned as his valet and ask him how to find her, but that would probably be a quicker way of advertising his intent than using the phone. He could prowl the passages of the silent palace, hoping for a miracle…

But then he saw that he wouldn't need to. Rosie appeared at the French windows through which she had disappeared on that first day and walked quickly across the cobbles on the far side of the courtyard.

His heart bumped in his chest. Even in the dim evening light her beauty shone. Her hair flowed down her back in waves, briefly gleaming in a shaft of light shed by a lantern on the wall. Her slim form, swathed in a shawl, moved with easy grace as she approached the archway, and then she paused and looked back over her shoulder.

Luca stood stock-still, holding his breath, wondering if she would see him. But she slipped into the darkness of the archway and disappeared.

Without making a conscious decision, Rosa's feet took her towards the rose-covered arbour in the far corner of the garden where she'd tried, unsuccessfully, to avoid Luca earlier in the week. It felt like a lifetime ago.

From the arbour she could look out over the flower garden, bordered with shrub roses, where she'd picked the flowers for her sister's wedding bouquet. If she couldn't talk to Sofia, this was the next best thing. She could remember every bloom she'd chosen, from the pink and creamy roses with their satiny petals and light, fresh scent, to the sweet jasmine and clean, woody lavender. There'd been daisies for simplicity and gypsophilia for delicacy, while the perfume of sweet peas had been strong and heady.

In the evening light she could barely see the terraces of flowers, but the mingled scents that wafted up to her on the warm air made her feel closer to Sofia. She settled herself on the cushions of the swing seat, pulled off her plimsols and wrapped the soft shawl around her shoulders.

The rhythmic swaying of the seat was soothing. She let her eyes close while she breathed in the perfumed air and felt the peace of the garden surround her.

'Rosie?'

She jerked upright, her brief moment of tranquillity shattered, and her fists closed on the edges of her shawl, pulling it tightly around her. But then her muscles relaxed and her shock drained away. This wasn't her father, or one of his emissaries come to find her.

Only one person called her by that name. It felt right, and not at all surprising, that it was Luca, even though when she'd walked away from him earlier she'd believed she would never see him again.

She turned her head against the cushions. 'How did you know where to find me?'

He moved closer, a defined shadow in the twilight. 'I saw you crossing the courtyard from my window. Finding you here was a lucky first guess.'

'You didn't think of trying the maze?'

'Luckily not. I'd be wandering its paths until morning. May I sit next to you?'

'Of course. Why…?'

'I had to see you, Rosie. There's something I need to explain.'

He sat, leaving space between them. She tucked her feet up under the skirt of her dress and turned a little. His sharp jaw looked cleanly shaven, and his dark eyes gleamed in what little light there was. Her heart did the little leap and then beat painfully against her ribs, just as it always did when he was near.

'Have you spoken to your father?' He sought out one of her hands and folded it in his.

'No. I'll have to talk to him tomorrow. Why?'

'I rather lost it with him, after you left earlier. I felt so impressed with how you managed the situation. You were right to walk away. I was also angry with him, and I should have let myself calm down, but I didn't.'

'What happened?' Her voice was a whisper. He wished he could freeze time and remain here with her like this for ever. But he had to tell her.

'I walked away before it became too heated. But I'll meet with him in the morning.' He pressed his mouth to her palm. 'I want to tell you before I see him...'

'What?'

'That I cannot marry you.'

He heard the hitch in her breathing. The silence around them seemed to gather and thicken. Then her breath stuttered. 'Why?'

He hated that he was going to hurt her.

'This proposed marriage feels like a trap my father set for me and, although he didn't know he was going to die, it's as if he's trying to control me from beyond the grave. As if he's scored a final victory over me, after all the times I defied him.'

He could feel useless anger towards his father building in his chest. 'I can never comply with it. I came here intending to tell your father to go to hell, and then—'

'Why didn't you?' Her voice rose. 'Why didn't you tell him as soon as you arrived?' She twisted towards him. 'Then none of this...'

'Believe me, that was my intention. I could have done it by email, but I thought I should meet your father. After all, it's something he's been counting on for twenty years. It seemed only good manners to tell him, man-to-man. I thought it would take a couple of hours.' His breath caught. 'But then I met you. I didn't think I would. It didn't seem necessary, but there you were, and I remembered you from twenty years ago...'

'How did *that* change anything? Surely meeting me simply confirmed that you were right to refuse to marry me?'

'Don't, Rosie, please. Don't let what your father has told you all your life become what defines you. You're so much better than that. You're worth so much more.'

'All I've ever been told is that nobody will desire or love me, so how else could I be? I had to wait to be married to someone—*you*—to cement a business transaction between two men who cared nothing for me. That *is* what has defined my life.'

He could hear the tremble in her voice and knew she was fighting to keep tears back.

'All you have to do is make sure I have a son to satisfy my father's obsessive need for an heir.'

'Shh, Rosie, listen to me—how much do you know about the agreement they made?'

Her shoulders jerked on a sob.

'Absolutely nothing. Like I told you, I didn't even know your name until I met you.'

'So you don't know that if we honoured that agreement should you—we—have a son, then when he is two years old we would have to relinquish him to live here, with your father, to be raised as his heir?'

Her head jerked round.

'What?'

'I didn't read the full agreement until after I'd arrived here, otherwise I don't think I would have paid your father the courtesy of a visit. Even if I didn't care about my father's actions, I could never go through with it under those terms. My mother died when I was two and I was sent to live with my grandparents. Then on my tenth birthday, with no warning, I was taken back to the estate in Tuscany to be brought up by my father. I will never, ever subject a child of mine to an experience like that.'

'I'm sorry, Luca. I didn't know.' She shivered. 'To lose your mother so young... Of course you'd never agree to give up a child of your own. I... can understand your reasons for refusing to comply with the agreement. But were your grandparents kind?'

'Yes, but they lived in a house belonging to my father and were bound to do what he wanted. I can see how he would have thought a marriage of convenience, which would bring him assets and a link to royalty, would be perfectly acceptable.'

'I still don't understand why you didn't just tell my father immediately.'

'Like I said, I met you.

'And I wasn't prepared to like you.

'I met you, Rosie, and I felt as if I'd found something incredibly rare and precious. I wanted to get to know you. I remembered what a bright, happy little girl you were. I wanted to discover what had changed you so much.'

He reached out to brush the backs of his fingers across her cheek. 'And why you no longer sing to the fish. I thought you'd probably been waiting for most of your life to meet me, be married and have children, and I was going to destroy all those dreams. I've meant every single one of the things I've said to you, but...'

He shook his head. 'I cannot agree to the terms of this deal. I wanted to find a way to tell you gently that I couldn't give you what you want. What you need.' He stroked a hand over her hair. 'But, instead, I've fallen in love with you.'

Rosa's mind threatened to spin out of control, unable to absorb what he was saying. She needed air, space, time, but there wasn't any. Luca had said he loved her, but he couldn't marry her and was leaving tomorrow...and she needed to show him that she loved him too, even though they could never be together.

He twisted to face her as his free hand brushed her hair off her face and cradled her cheek. He rubbed his thumb over her bottom lip. It only took the slightest turn of her head to press her mouth to his palm. His skin tasted clean and smelled of soap. She thought hazily that he must have showered the salt away, as she had done.

She pictured him in the shower, water cascading over those sculpted muscles of his chest and shoulders, running down his washboard stomach, and something clenched and snapped inside her. The longing to feel his skin against hers, with nothing between them, was overwhelmingly powerful. She wanted to make another memory to store away.

After tonight, he'd be gone from her life. Once

he'd broken off their engagement, her father would never permit him to return to Palosia, even if he wanted to come back. And, whatever Luca said about her finding someone else, no-one else would ever love her. At this moment, in the sweet-smelling darkness, she wanted to know how it felt to give herself completely to the man she loved.

She felt his fingers slide into her hair, cradling the back of her head as he leaned into her.

'Luca…'

'Mmm?' His forehead rested against hers, his fingers feathering across her cheeks and down to her collar bones, easing the edges of the pashmina apart and probing the sensitive places of her neck and throat.

'Make love to me. Please.'

Luca stilled, aware that his breathing was growing uneven and aware of the fragility of the grip he had on his control. He needed to stop this, but overriding all his thoughts was the deep, visceral need to make her his. It expanded from somewhere deep in his core and obliterated sense and logic.

His awareness shrank to this place, this moment and the feel of Rosie's soft curves, the scent of her skin and the small sounds of need in her throat. He wanted to kiss her so that, if she ever kissed another man, she would think of *him*. If anyone else ever touched her, it would be the imprint of *his* fingers she remembered and longed for.

Because he loved her. It was the only thing in this tangled web that made any sense.

'Rosie, no...'

'Please, Luca. This is the only chance I'll have... *we'll* have. Please, kiss me.'

He pulled in a shaky breath. 'You're lovely. You're absolutely enchanting and I want you more than anything I've ever longed for or desired.' He brushed his mouth across her lips and drew back again as she arched towards him, her head falling back, the creamy skin of her throat a soft gleam in the half-dark. Her eyelids closed over her shiny eyes.

He cupped her head in his hands, holding her steady while he kissed her again, more firmly, opening the seam of her lips with his and sliding his tongue into the sweet warmth of her mouth. It was heaven. Hell would come later, when he had to leave her.

Her hands were buried in his hair as she kissed him back, and then he broke away from her mouth to drop a line of light kisses across her shoulder and along the neckline of her cotton dress to the shadowy dip between her breasts. He heard her soft gasp and reached up to stroke her cheek.

'We can stop, Rosie. Just tell me...' He wasn't

sure how he'd stop, but he'd find a way. He would never do anything she didn't want, or anything to hurt her. She was precious and beautiful, and he wanted with all his heart and soul to protect her, and *love* her, for ever.

'I want this,' she whispered. 'I want you. Now. Because, when you're gone, I'll always have this to remember.'

He raised his head and found her mouth again.

Afterwards, he held her in his arms as their breathing calmed and, after thundering against each other, their hearts quietened.

He'd hesitated, then covered her mouth with his when she'd cried out, hating that he'd hurt her, but she'd pulled him closer again. Then his name had become a mantra that she'd breathed over and over, until finally it had become one sharp cry of pleasure, followed by his own groan of release.

She shivered and he pulled her shawl over them. Later the air chilled with a dewy dampness, and he helped her to dress. Then he eased her onto his lap and held her close again, her head tucked into his shoulder.

'I'm sorry.'

She struggled upright, away from him, pushing her hands against his chest. His fingers looped lightly around her wrists.

'Sorry? How can you be sorry, Luca? I wanted you and I think you wanted me.'

'Rosie, listen to me. Please.'

She wriggled off his lap. Her legs felt weak. Luca stood too, towering over her, holding her hands against his chest. 'Tell me why you're sorry.'

'I'm not sorry that we made love. It was beautiful.' There was a crack in his voice. 'More than beautiful. I love you and I'm sorry that I can't marry you.'

Rosa slid her hands from under his, even though she longed to keep them there.

'I've felt so safe with you, Luca, but suddenly nothing about this feels safe.'

'Rosie.' His voice was quiet, insistent. 'I love you, yet I cannot marry you under the terms of the agreement our fathers made. If I could find a way for us to be together, free from these obligations...'

She shook her head. 'I don't want a marriage that's been pre-arranged for the convenient satisfaction of two massive male egos either, even if one of them is no longer with us. Have you thought about how it looks from my point of view?'

'Yes, of course I have.'

'Then can you tell me how a marriage of convenience could ever become a love match?'

She'd seen both her father's marriages fail when no heir had been born, her parents becoming lonely and embittered. Sofia's mother had loved her, but she'd left her as a baby to return to her first love. For much of her life, Rosa had feared that her own mother would leave and return to her family. She didn't know if Chiara loved her enough to stay, because she knew she was unlovable. How could she bear it if her childhood fears came true, and someone who professed to love her abandoned her?

'Because if we were free to choose each other it wouldn't be a marriage of convenience, Rosie. It'd be a marriage filled with love.'

Doubt and fear crowded in on her. It could never be the sort of union she dreamed about, like the one between Sofia and Marco. The past would always cast a shadow over them. It was much safer to be on her own. On her own, she'd have control of her life, even if it was narrow. She wouldn't have to fear not having a son, or being left for someone else, or leaving her mother unprotected.

Yet would it be worth it, if a way could be found? Did she dare to believe that might be possible? She needed to be on her own, to have space to think. Luca's presence made that impossible. The longer she stood so close to him, his male scent filling her senses, his hard body now promising so much more than security and comfort, the more likely she was to believe in what he said.

'I need to go, Luca.' She finally found the will to drag the words out of herself.

'I'm afraid to let you go, Rosie.' His voice shook.

Hot tears scalded her eyes. Those few words, spoken with such a depth of feeling and emotion, told her more about his love for her than anything else. But she couldn't take the risk. He'd made her feel valued and precious, and had made love to her with such gentleness and passion that she'd treasure the memories for ever. But she had to remember what she would tell her father tomorrow: she would never marry anyone unless they loved each other equally and deeply. And she couldn't allow herself to believe, absolutely, that the love Luca promised would be for ever.

She shook her head. 'And I'm afraid to stay,' she whispered. She took a step backwards. 'It could never work, Luca. There's too much in our past to allow us to have a future together.'

Then she turned and began to run.

A shadow fell across the earth where Rosa was digging. The flower bed had already been weeded and dug over once, but physically exhausting herself was the only way she could think of to cope with the grief that overwhelmed her every time she stopped to rest. She'd wrestled with it all night, unable to shake the conviction that she'd let something very precious slip away.

She stood up, wiping her hands on her thighs, and faced her father.

'He's gone.' He sounded breathless, seething. 'He's broken the agreement his father made with me.'

Despite the amount of cold water she'd splashed on her face earlier, she knew the signs of sadness and a sleep-deprived night were obvious but, since her father rarely looked at her, properly, it was unlikely he'd notice. For once, she felt grateful for his indifference.

She lifted her shoulders a little. 'Yes.'

Her father's eyes narrowed. 'You knew? Did he speak to you? What did he say?'

He looked curiously diminished, haggard and slightly stooped. This morning, Luisa had hinted at the eruption of uncomplimentary comments about King Fiero on social media. The people were calling for change, she'd muttered, before hurrying away.

This might be her fault, but perhaps in the end it would be for the good of Palosia if it instigated that change. Her father had been impervious to criticism all his life, but perhaps he was feeling the heat at last.

'He said he couldn't marry me, but that shouldn't surprise you.'

'Obviously you didn't please him, for him to give up all that you would have brought him.' He scowled.

'He's a man who is highly successful in his own right. He needs none of the trappings, or the problems, that marrying me would bring. He has everything he wants without that.'

'And it doesn't bother you, that you've squandered the chance to provide Palosia with an heir?'

For the first time in her life, she stared him down. 'No, it doesn't, especially since, if you had your way, that heir would be taken from me at the age of two to be raised by you. Did you believe you would get away with that? A solitary future doesn't scare me at all, but the idea of a loveless marriage of convenience is terrifying. I will *only* marry for love.'

'*Love*,' he spat. 'What do you know of love? Your half-sister's marriage has filled your head with fantasies.'

'No. It has shown me that a marriage of equal love and respect between two people is possible and, above all, joyful.'

She turned and walked away. She felt no urge to look back. Instead, a sense of liberation filled her, lightening her step and even lifting her heart a little.

CHAPTER SEVENTEEN

LUCA FROWNED AND dropped his phone onto his desk.

He'd known hell would come later, but he hadn't expected the pain to intensify rather than diminish as the days passed. He'd thought getting back into his life in New York would make the memory of events on Palosia fade. Instead, they were sharper than ever.

He'd worked for two weeks solid, and his brain felt fried. The hit he usually got from success in court had failed to deliver and, instead of feeling happy at the latest victory, he was simply exhausted. Add to that the fact that he couldn't get hold of Rosie, and he was setting himself up for a major all-fall-down.

This morning he'd snapped at his PA when she'd brought him coffee, exactly the way he liked it, and suggested he might take a break.

'What would I do with a break? Any useful suggestions?'

Her eyebrows had disappeared beneath her glossy fringe but she hadn't answered.

Later, however, he'd found a brochure for high-end spa breaks in the Caribbean on his desk. He'd dropped it in the bin.

He pushed away from his desk, strode to the expanse of glass that was his office window and looked out at the iconic skyline. The buzz of New York no longer fired him up. Instead of skyscrapers and Central Park, he wanted mountains, beaches and...

He didn't need a spa break. He just needed to speak to Rosie and know that she was okay. Then he could move on.

What if her father had blamed her for the way Luca had cancelled their engagement and was meting out some sort of punishment? Had her phone been confiscated, leaving her with no means of talking to anyone, not even her beloved sister? How would she cope with that? Every time he tried to call her, he was met with silence. He was a breath away from throwing the phone at something—or someone.

It was his job to defend people, stand up for their rights and speak for them, when necessary. He told himself he needed to do that for Rosie, but then, judging by the way he'd seen her face down her father, perhaps she no longer needed his help.

But if he was honest, which he always was, speaking to her would never be enough. The depth of his longing for her touch, her kiss, just *her*, was bottomless and beyond the realm of all his previous experience. As a result, he had no idea how to deal with it, and his frustration was building with every day, every hour, which passed.

For the first time since he'd freed himself from his father's control all those years ago, he felt dissatisfied with his life. He wanted something different. The admission shook him. He'd glimpsed heaven in Rosie's arms on Palosia and he craved more of it.

He was in love, for the first time ever. Love was meant to bring joy, he thought, but it was agony. He thought he'd be able to get back to work and park the tumultuous emotions he was experiencing somewhere safe, to be visited when he felt better equipped to examine them. But that wasn't how it had worked. They ruled his life, waking and sleeping. Everything reminded him of her and he knew, with absolute certainty, that he wanted her in his life full-time.

He'd told Rosie he loved her, but in the next breath told her why he couldn't marry her. His reasons were sound, and he'd never change his mind about them, but how it must have hurt her—made her doubt his sincerity, believe that cruel nonsense that she was unlovable. She'd pushed him away, panicked and fled. That he hadn't gone after her was an error that would haunt him for ever.

He needed to speak to her, desperately. He pressed the heels of his hands into his eyes, but immediately imagined her standing in front of him in her gardening clothes and hat, giving him that rare smile that made him want to kiss her and which he'd pay a king's ransom to see again.

Something connected in his tired brain. If he wanted to see her smile—see *her*, damn it— he had to stop wishing. He retrieved his phone from across the desk and scrolled through his diary and commitments. There was nothing that couldn't be handled by someone else for the coming week, because he only employed the best.

He sent a request to the travel department and buzzed his PA.

She came in, looking mutinous. 'If you're going to…'

He held up a hand. 'I'm really sorry about earlier. I'm not myself.'

'I don't need you to tell me that. You've been like a bear with a sore head ever since you returned from Italy. Your father's death has affected you deeply.'

'Yes, it has.' *If only you knew.* 'And I've decided to take your advice. I'm taking a break.

But, before I disappear, please get one of the partners in the Rome office on the line. I have something unusual for them to tackle…'

Looking back and wishing that things were different was a waste of time and energy. Besides, there were things for which Rosa was grateful. The groundswell of opinion in Palosia towards allowing a female to succeed to the throne was one of them. It seemed her father had finally, and reluctantly, bowed to public pressure and might consider initiating changes in the ancient laws. It wouldn't happen overnight but it had to be a good thing for their small kingdom.

The inner strength that she'd found with Luca had not deserted her. She felt as if it had always been there, waiting for the right moment to show itself, and his kind attention had been the catalyst.

She also felt the beginnings of tolerance for her father. In making her choice, she'd removed any leverage he had over her. She could protect her mother and increase the amount of charity work she undertook. It was fulfilling and rewarding.

But she hadn't yet learned to limit the scope of her imagination or her emotions. The gut-twisting longing persisted. A spotlight seemed to shine on the memories of Luca, illuminating those few days, picking them out in vivid Technicolor. Every word they'd spoken, every touch, every sigh, was imprinted on her memory. The memories showed no sign of fading or losing the ability to wring her heart.

A phrase, a scent, the taste of salt on her tongue... There was no telling when she'd be hit with longing so powerful that she gasped.

Finally, longing for the comfort of her sister's voice, she called her from the hat factory.

'What's happened, Rosa? Why doesn't your phone work? And you sound...different.'

There would be no use denying it, and it was a relief to be able to talk about Luca. Sofia listened in silence as Rosa told her everything...well, not exactly *everything*.

'And he said he loved you?' Rosa heard the change in Sofia's tone. 'Since you're the most lovable person on the planet, I'm not surprised. Whatever our father says.'

'But I didn't know whether to believe him or not.'

'Why would he say it if it wasn't true?'

'I don't know. I was shocked and confused. He said he couldn't submit to a marriage of convenience, but he wished there was another way.'

'He's right about the agreement, Rosa, and it was honourable of him to be honest with you. So I don't believe he was lying when he said he loved you. What did you say?'

'I said it would never work. I didn't see how it could. The past would always intrude.'

'You could choose to let the past go. If the agreement was cancelled, you could start afresh. Love is one of the most powerful things in the world, and with the love of a good man your life would be transformed. After all, I know. And it sounds to me as if Luca is a good man. He's prepared to stand up for what is right, in his professional and his personal life.'

Rosa gripped the phone more tightly, squeezing her eyes tighter still. 'I should have told him...' Her voice caught.

'What, sweet sister?'

The endearment, always loved, now made her want to cry.

'That I love him too.'

'You *didn't*?'

'No. I tried to...*show* him. But my feelings frightened me. I felt so vulnerable.'

Sofia was silent for a moment. When she spoke again, there was added weight to her voice. 'Rosa, you once told me that it's good for people to know they are loved. Do you remember?'

'Y...yes, I do.'

'And you said Marco deserved the truth. Your wise words that day changed everything for me... for us. They granted me the clarity to see what I needed to do. Marco and I are eternally grateful to you.' Rosa heard the wobble in her sister's voice, but then Sofia continued. 'Now you need to take your own advice. Can you contact Luca?'

'He has my number.' She remembered the phone lying in her bureau drawer, the battery dead. 'But I don't have his. And I turned my phone off after he left and let the battery die.'

'Okay...' There was a grim note in Sofia's voice. 'I lost count of how many times I tried to phone you after those photos appeared on social media. How do you know Luca hasn't been trying to contact you?'

'Why would he?'

'Because he *loves* you,' Sofia said gently. 'Love isn't something you can switch off when it suits you, like your phone. Charge it and switch it on, Rosa.'

That conversation had been two days ago. She'd followed Sofia's advice, but her phone remained silent. Despite her determination to ignore the steady march of time, she knew it had been three weeks and two days since Luca had left.

Impatient with herself, she threw off the bed covers and pulled open the curtains at the window. The sky was a deep, velvet blue quilted with stars, and she knew the air would have the crispness that came with September, heralding the earliest signs of autumn.

She pulled on a dress and then picked up the pashmina she'd left folded on a chair for the past three weeks, allowing herself a moment to bury her face in its soft folds, because in her mind it still held Luca's clean, soapy smell.

Then she let herself out into the garden.

Luca pulled the hire car off the road and into the layby. The rush of silence when he cut the engine seemed almost tangible after the constant, twenty-four-hour cacophony of the city that never slept.

He remembered the code for the locked gate after having watched Rosie punch it in, but he still felt a rush of relief when the gate clicked open. The grass beneath the fruit trees cushioned his footsteps as he climbed steadily up the terraces.

Above him crouched the silhouette of the palace, light illuminating a few windows. He didn't know how he'd find Rosie, but he was determined that he would.

He paused where two paths crossed, debating which one to choose, and then he heard a sound that simultaneously tore at his heart and sent it soaring. The maze was dark on this moonless night. He kept one hand on the spiky hedge to guide him through its twists and turns.

At the centre, he stopped. A clear, sweet voice singing about pretty horses floated on the night air.

'Rosie?'

Her voice wavered and died. Starlight glimmered off the cascade of her hair as she turned.

'Luca?'

He closed the space between them in three strides.

'I came to find you.' He stopped, afraid to touch her in case he frightened her away. 'I had to know that you're alright. I've tried to contact you...'

She put out a hand and touched his chest.

'The phone felt like a trap, and I didn't think you'd want to contact me after what I said. So I switched it off. But Sofia persuaded me to turn it on again, just two days ago.'

'I gave up trying to call you. I decided to come to Palosia instead. And you were right—there *is* too much in our past, and we can't erase it, but the marriage deal is being dissolved. We'll be free of it, free to do as we choose.'

'Yes, I demanded that my father cancel his side of the agreement and the notion about handing an heir to him. I told him I choose to remain single. I choose to help the people of Palosia through my charity work, and to help protect the unique habitats of our precious island. And I'd never choose to marry for convenience. Only for love.'

The need to touch her after these weeks of missing her became too much and he reached out, taking her hands. 'I choose you.'

She stilled, her dark eyes luminous. 'Luca.' She breathed his name. 'That last night...it's tormented me.'

Fear that she was going to say she regretted their lovemaking gripped him. 'I'm sorry, Rosie. I should have been restrained. I hurt you.'

'No. I should have told you what I'd been wanting to tell you.'

He searched her face. 'What should you have told me?'

'That I love you. But I couldn't see how we could make something new and beautiful out of our past.'

He pulled her against him, kissing her hair and then resting his forehead against hers. 'I've missed you every minute we've been apart, with every cell of my body, and I've been so afraid for you. I had to come and find you.' He kissed her, slowly and gently.

'How did you know where to find me?' she asked when he lifted his lips from hers.

'I didn't. I heard you singing. You've found your voice.'

'Yes, I have. And I'll never be silenced again.'

He smiled against her mouth. 'The courage

you showed, facing your father, was inspiring. It made me realise that I was being a coward.'

'But it was you who gave me the strength to stand up to my father.'

He shook his head. 'I was afraid of love. I feared that my mother hadn't loved me enough, or my father at all, and my grandparents only from a sense of obligation. I refused to acknowledge my true feelings for you and, when I did, I told you that I couldn't marry you. My obsession with refusing to allow my father to control my life clouded the truth. But I realised that, if I denied my love for you, he would have scored the ultimate victory. He'd have stopped me from being with the only woman in the world I want. I'm not letting that happen.'

'Does this mean that our twenty-year engagement is over?'

'Mmm. Do you think we can start again?'

'What do you mean?'

'I've made a career out of trying to improve the lives of others, but I've been afraid to examine my own. Acknowledging that I love you makes me feel vulnerable, but I do—unconditionally and completely. I'd love you just the same if you were the gardener I mistook you for, and not the daughter of a king. I love you for your generosity of spirit and your kindness and care for others. I'll care for you and protect you for ever. There're no certainties in life, and we'll have challenges to face, but I'll be by your side through anything… if you'll marry me.'

'Oh, Luca. Yes.' The raw emotion in her voice made his chest ache. 'I was so afraid of loving you. But your love has given me the courage to love you back without fear. We can love each other freely, on our own terms. You, and your love, are safe with me.'

Their kiss was deep and long. Luca trailed his fingers over her shoulders to span her narrow waist in his hands, holding her hips against him.

'Do you think your father is still awake?' he whispered when they broke apart. 'Because I think we need to tell him our plans.'

'He may be, but tomorrow will be soon enough to tell him. We can keep tonight for ourselves.'

'In that case, I have to ask something of you.'

'What?'

'To lead me out of the maze—because without you I'll be lost for ever.'

Rosie laughed and took his hand. 'Come; I'll show you how easy it is.'

'And then I'll show you how easy it is to love you. Over and over again—for ever.'

EPILOGUE

Rosa scanned the congregation in the palace chapel. Everyone wore a smile—even her father. Seated beside him, her mother looked happy too.

All of Marco's big family was there, and her heart swelled, knowing that Sofia had been welcomed into their midst with such warm generosity.

They had all gathered for the baptism of one-month-old Angelica Sofia Rosabella, Sofia and Marco's daughter, and the atmosphere in the chapel hummed with joy.

Sofia and Marco wore the happiest smiles of all. They stood at the carved marble font, and Sofia cradled their perfect baby girl in her arms. Downy, dark hair curled at the edges of her lace bonnet, and her grey eyes, just like her father's, gazed up unblinkingly at her parents. Sofia rocked her gently, smoothing the silk christening robe that had been worn by generations of royal babies of Palosia.

Rosa's eyes caught Sofia's, and they exchanged a warm smile.

Sofia had kept her hair short, and Rosa loved the way the glossy bob curved along her jaw as she bent her head over her baby daughter. When Marco had taken Sofia to his villa on Capri to hide from the men King Fiero had sent to find her, he'd cut her long hair into a bob as part of her disguise.

The King had surprised everyone by being besotted with his baby granddaughter. He insisted that she be christened on Palosia and that, even though they lived in Italy, Sofia and Marco should have a home on the island. It was as if, confronted by the reality of a new generation, he was able to see his own place in the world more clearly, and accept that there were some things he couldn't control.

As for the things he could, he was doing something about them. He was changing the law of succession so that a woman could rule. He had officially recognised the valuable contribution Queen Chiara had made to the lives of the people of Palosia, and agreed to support the movement that advocated tertiary education equally for girls and boys.

Much remained to be done, and for Rosa her relationship with him would always be difficult, but her generous spirit allowed her to regard him with increasing tolerance.

Luca's hand brushed against hers and she entwined her fingers with his, feeling that current of strength, security and love—so much love—that his touch always brought her.

They had been married seven months ago in the private chapel of Luca's castle in Tuscany. They hadn't wanted a grand wedding, happy to make their vows in the company of family and a few trusted friends.

The bodice of Rosa's antique ivory silk wedding dress had hugged her curves then fallen in liquid folds to the floor, sparkling with gems and gleaming seed pearls.

When Luca had lifted her veil, his eyes had shone unnaturally brightly, and a muscle in his jaw had flexed. 'My love,' he'd whispered, taking her hand.

Her engagement ring was tucked safely in a pocket of Luca's suit, ready to return to her as soon as he'd slipped her wedding band onto her finger. She'd missed the weight and sparkle of its rose-pink diamonds.

They'd invited Queen Chiara to move to Tuscany with them, but she'd refused. Her place was on Palosia, she'd said. With Rosa leaving, she'd have to pay more attention to her charities and gardens. Her selfless demonstration of loyalty and service had helped to motivate King Fiero to initiate change, both in his public and personal life.

Luca bent his head towards Rosa. 'Are you alright? Not feeling tired?'

The wide smile she gave him was the one he always craved. His hand tightened around hers.

'I'm fine. But thank you for your concern.'

He dipped his head further and brushed his lips across her temple. 'Nothing is more precious to me than you. And now…'

She nodded, because the service was about to begin and there was no more time for words. But the understanding between them needed none. They had their own very precious secret that they would keep for a few weeks yet. They didn't know if their baby would be a boy or a girl, but they knew that one day he or she would rule Palosia with the blessing of the people.

Their hearts were full to overflowing with love.

* * * * *

If you missed the previous story in the Princesses of Palosia duet, then check out
Secret Royal's Napoli Reunion *by Nina Milne*

And if you enjoyed this story, check out these other great reads from Suzanne Merchant

Best Man's Second Chance
Cinderella's Adventure with the CEO
Heiress's Escape to South Africa

All available now!

Get up to 4 Free Books!

We'll send you 2 free books from each series you try PLUS a free Mystery Gift.

FREE Value Over $25

Both the **Harlequin® Historical** and **Harlequin® Romance** series feature compelling novels filled with emotion and simmering romance.

YES! Please send me 2 FREE novels from the Harlequin Historical or Harlequin Romance series and my FREE Mystery Gift (gift is worth about $10 retail). After receiving them, if I don't wish to receive any more books, I can return the shipping statement marked "cancel." If I don't cancel, I will receive 5 brand-new Harlequin Historical books every month and be billed just $6.39 each in the U.S. or $7.19 each in Canada, or 4 brand-new Harlequin Romance Larger-Print books every month and be billed just $7.19 each in the U.S. or $7.99 each in Canada, a savings of 20% off the cover price. It's quite a bargain! Shipping and handling is just 50¢ per book in the U.S. and $1.25 per book in Canada.* I understand that accepting the 2 free books and gift places me under no obligation to buy anything. I can always return a shipment and cancel at any time by calling the number below. The free books and gift are mine to keep no matter what I decide.

Choose one:
☐ **Harlequin Historical** (246/349 BPA G36Y)
☐ **Harlequin Romance Larger-Print** (119/319 BPA G36Y)
☐ **Or Try Both!** (246/349 & 119/319 BPA G36Z)

Name (please print)

Address   Apt. #

City   State/Province   Zip/Postal Code

Email: Please check this box ☐ if you would like to receive newsletters and promotional emails from Harlequin Enterprises ULC and its affiliates. You can unsubscribe anytime.

Mail to the Harlequin Reader Service:
IN U.S.A.: P.O. Box 1341, Buffalo, NY 14240-8531
IN CANADA: P.O. Box 603, Fort Erie, Ontario L2A 5X3

Want to explore our other series or interested in ebooks? Visit www.ReaderService.com or call 1-800-873-8635.

---

*Terms and prices subject to change without notice. Prices do not include sales taxes, which will be charged (if applicable) based on your state or country of residence. Canadian residents will be charged applicable taxes. Offer not valid in Quebec. This offer is limited to one order per household. Books received may not be as shown. Not valid for current subscribers to the Harlequin Historical or Harlequin Romance series. All orders subject to approval. Credit or debit balances in a customer's account(s) may be offset by any other outstanding balance owed by or to the customer. Please allow 4 to 6 weeks for delivery. Offer available while quantities last.

Your Privacy—Your information is being collected by Harlequin Enterprises ULC, operating as Harlequin Reader Service. For a complete summary of the information we collect, how we use this information and to whom it is disclosed, please visit our privacy notice located at https://corporate.harlequin.com/privacy-notice. Notice to California Residents – Under California law, you have specific rights to control and access your data. For more information on these rights and how to exercise them, visit https://corporate.harlequin.com/california-privacy. For additional information for residents of other U.S. states that provide their residents with certain rights with respect to personal data, visit https://corporate.harlequin.com/other-state-residents-privacy-rights/.